John Habberton

The Annals of a Baby

How it Was Named, how it Was Nursed, how it Was a Tyrant, and how its Nose Got

out of Joint

John Habberton

The Annals of a Baby
How it Was Named, how it Was Nursed, how it Was a Tyrant, and how its Nose Got out of Joint

ISBN/EAN: 9783337157470

Printed in Europe, USA, Canada, Australia, Japan

Cover: Foto ©Andreas Hilbeck / pixelio.de

More available books at **www.hansebooks.com**

THE ANNALS
OF A BABY.

A COMPANION TO "HELEN'S BABIES."

THE ANNALS
OF A BABY.

HOW IT WAS NAMED; HOW IT WAS NURSED; HOW IT WAS A TYRANT; AND HOW ITS NOSE GOT OUT OF JOINT.

ALSO,

A FEW WORDS ABOUT ITS AUNTIES, ITS GRANDFATHERS, GRAND-MOTHERS, AND OTHER IMPORTANT RELATIONS.

BY

ONE OF ITS SLAVES.

NEW YORK:

G. W. Carleton & Co., Publishers.

LONDON: S. LOW & CO.

CONTENTS.

PAGE

I.—Baby's First Gifts...................................:. 7

II.—Naming the Baby............................... 24

III.—One of The Aunties.............................. 43

IV.—Baby's Nurse...................................... 58

V.—The Crippled Sister............................. 93

VI.—Baby's Party.................................... 124

VII.—The Sunset of Life.............................. 154

VIII.—Aunt Hannah..................................... 166

IX.—Baby's Nose is out of Joint...................... 206

X.—Passing Away..................................... 215

THE ANNALS OF A BABY.

———•◆•———

I.

BABY'S FIRST GIFTS.

ONCE upon a time a Baby was born in a happy home, where the Father and Mother were young, and where there were no other children. It was a soft, pink little thing, with just dark, downy rings for hair, and a sound like a bird's chirrup for its first weak human cry. There was great joy in the house about it; every one who saw it said there never was such a baby before, and never could be such another. Its Mother had held it a moment on her arm, looking at it in a wonder that it could be really hers, and with a gush of strange love that stirred great shining tears into her eyes, which would have fallen on the Baby, only the

Fat Nurse with the frilled cap snatched it away and
told her "it was unlucky to cry over a new-born child!"
The Father had stolen into the room on tiptoe, kissed
his pale girl-wife with a deeper tenderness than he had
ever yet felt, had awkwardly held the tiny, warm roll
in his strong hands as if it was glass that he was afraid
of breaking, and had then been sent away like a victim
into outer regions. The Grandfathers had come, leaning on their gold-headed canes. They smiled at each
other, and shook hands across the narrow white crib ;
and as they joked over the Baby there was a faint sigh
smothered down by each at their own gray hairs, and
a little sadness they did not show as they thought of
the trials of life that surely lay before that untried
soul. The Grandmothers, in their black silk dresses,
and with nice rosy faces, had smoothed it and patted it
and half cried over it, talking all the while about the
births of their own babies that were grown up men and
women now, and feeling as if this Baby was a born
princess and they both queen-dowagers. And all the
Young Aunties, with their gay floating ribbons and
fancy aprons, had fluttered in groups around the sleep-
ing stranger, had held up their dimpled hands in

delight, and kissed it softly in subdued ecstasies; called it "a rosebud," "a seraph," and many other endearing titles; quarrelled who should take it first and hold it longest, until they also had been cleared out, like other victims, by the fat old woman with the frilled cap, who seemed to consider the Baby as her own special possession. The youngest of the Aunties said she was "a bear"—behind her back, however; and the oldest of the Young Aunties held her head up very high, and wondered "who the darling would be named after."

Every one who came brought the Baby a present, until there never was a baby who had so many and such different gifts. Its own crib, its mother's bed, and its pretty dressing-basket were piled full of them; and the Baby lay in the midst on its snowy pillow, quite careless of all these tokens of affection and admiration; able, in fact, to do nothing but rest after the weariness of being born into the world. There were all sorts of rattles and whistles, and india-rubber balls covered with net, a big doll twice as large as Baby's self, with a satin dress and movable eyes, and a blue pincushion with "Baby" spelt on it in bright
1*

fresh pins intended for Baby's future torture. There
were also daintily embroidered slips worked by the
Aunties, finely wrought flannels that had tried aged
spectacles, silver spoons and forks to feed the pouting
mouth still sucking in sleep, and a gold cross and chain
that was laid upon the small breast which had scarcely
yet learned to heave with breath. Every one that
brought a gift brought also good wishes and bright
hopes and tender prayers for the innocent little life.
Only one Poor Relation brought all these without anything else; for she was one of those who are rich only
in love, and have nothing to spare from the hard-earned
daily bread that fed the hungry. She was not gay and
young like the Aunties; care and trials had taken
away her youth and gayety; but her heart yearned over
the Baby perhaps more earnestly than theirs. She was
sorry she could not bring something to the child of
more value than costly toys or dresses—some gift that
should be a talisman against pain and evil, something
a soul might prize through all eternity. She wished
she could summon the fairies, as was done in olden
times, to bestow gifts on the children of kings and
queens; only she shuddered when she remembered

that with the rest came always a malignant hag who vented her spite in a curse that counteracted all the good offerings of the others. Nevertheless, when she had kissed the Baby " good-by," and murmured a short prayer over it, she wended her way homeward with her head full of this same fancy, for the Poor Relation had a poet's heart, though she had never found time from work to sing a poet's songs, and she had secretly kept green there many a faith of her childhood. She could not help thinking, as she walked slowly over the fields, that if she could only find a five-leaved clover, and hold it in her hand in the open air at midnight, perhaps she would see the Fairy Court, and could ask the queen to shed her bounty on the dear infant. She stepped carefully over the grass, so as not to tread on the daisies—for she was almost as fond of flowers as of babies—and looked for the clover, though she smiled at herself for pretending to believe there were such mysterious creatures as fairies any more in this changed every-day world. She recollected how often she had hunted for a five-leaved clover when she was a little girl, all over these same meadows, down by the brook-side, and out in the still, solemn woods, and never had found one;

and she remembered also how many times she had been told there was no such growth in nature. After awhile, with a sad sigh, she gave up looking for it, and wished she was a child again, with nothing to do but wander under the trees, and run races with the sparkling rills. The sky was all crimson and gold with the sunset, and as she raised her head to gaze at the tinted clouds, she stumbled over a stone hidden in the grass; as she glanced down again, lo! before her she suddenly beheld the object of her search, a very and true clover with five leaves, just nestling under the shadow of a full-spread buttercup. She could scarcely believe her eyes, and almost trembled with a sort of awe as she broke it from its slender stalk, and then she was as glad as if she had really been only a child; she laughed over it, and talked to herself about what it should reveal to her, till pleasure brought a flush to her worn cheeks that made her look quite young and pretty, just as she did when she thought she should, perhaps, some day have babies of her own to love.

That night, before the clock struck twelve, when her Aged Father and Mother and her Crippled Sister were fast asleep, she slipped noiselessly down the stairs and

out on the open porch of her humble home, where the
moonlight was shining through the vines. She told herself that, at her age, it was silly to be playing such foolish pranks; but she held the five-leaved clover tight in
her hand, and stood under the arch of boughs, looking
out on the narrow lawn dotted with bushes, and waiting
for midnight. Just at the first stroke of the solemn
bell that always tolled the hours, a slight breeze stirred
all the leaves around her, and a sort of gentle rustling
floated on the quiet air; on the third stroke all the
flowers on the vines seemed to expand into full bloom,
and turned slowly towards the lawn; at the fifth, innumerable fire-flies gathered on that one spot; at the
seventh, the dew-drops appeared to grow hard and
glitter with brilliant rays like diamonds; at the ninth,
the roses shed floods of perfume, and the jessamine
stars fairly distilled a precious odor; at the eleventh
stroke a slender white circle glistened in front of her
as if the blades of grass had been bent and strung with
oriental pearls; and at the twelfth, there, suddenly before her, was the fairy court. The fairies were all
dressed in green, so that, if it had not been for their
bright little faces, she might not have thought them

fairies at all, but only leaves on the bushes. Titania was throned on a white rose just a petal or two higher than Puck, who was making faces at the train-bearers of her majesty as they stood just behind her; the rest were seated on the dew-drops, perched among the blossoms, or balancing on feathery sprays. Titania alone seemed to be arrayed in a silvery mist, with a crown of many-colored jewels on her head, each so small as to be only a spark, and with the breast-plume of a humming-bird in her hand for a sceptre. When she spoke, her voice was low, soft, and clear, like the singing of a far-off lark; the men fairies all pulled off their caps, and Puck stopped plaguing the pages, and turned his twinkling eyes upon her face as he listened.

"In the name of the five-leaved clover," she said, " the fairy Court has been summoned. The fairies can refuse nothing to the holder of this charm; make thy request of Titania."

The Poor Relation answered like one in a dream: " Gifts for a Baby, O Queen!"

The fairy swayed forward a little, and asked with tender interest: "Is it a Baby-boy, or a Baby-girl?" And when she heard the echo "A girl!" a sadness passed like a fleeting shadow over the brightness of her face, which, being noticed by Puck, he gave out a mocking laugh, like the whistle of an insect. But the queen waved her sceptre for silence, and a sort of sorrowing expression fell upon the countenances of all, even upon the brow of her sportive husband, while she spoke :

" Many years ago we could have brought this Baby rare offerings, that would have made all the world know that she had fairies for godmothers; but, with the belief of men in our power, much of our power is gone ; the gnomes and the elves have all died, so we have no more tribute from the earth and the mines; your electricity has desolated the water—kingdom of the sylphs, and we receive no longer the treasures of the seas; the salamanders are bound in their summer sleep, and the fickle sprites of air are not now in league with us."

Here the queen paled, and Puck swore a round oath, drawing his tiny sword, as a rough gale shook the flower on which they sat.

" But still," she resumed as the breeze passed, beaming at the Poor Relation like a star emerging from a cloud, "still, for those who come to us in faith the fairies have some gifts to render yet. There are not many of us left, and our rich jewels have been stolen from us one by one. It has been long since we have been called upon to bless a cradle, but this Baby shall have all the fairy store of presents. Offer first, O Puck, my lord the king!"

"Ho, ho!" said the merry monarch, nodding joyously to the Poor Relation, "I give the Baby something better than gems—a light heart and a free wit!"

"And I," said another, in answer to the queen, "I bestow a winning smile."

"And I a rose-hue on the cheeks."

"And I a soft hand in sickness, and a strong one to protect the weak."

Thus, one after another, the fairies chirped out their many gifts, till grace, modesty, tenderness, talent, and countless outward beauties had been showered on the unconscious Baby. The Poor Relation's heart was all in a glow and her eyes full of thankful drops to think what favor she had won for the child, when she had not been able to give it a rattle or a doll; and she was especially glad that all the bad fairies of old stories

had seemed to have died out, since not one evil wish
was expressed. But suddenly the five-leaved clover
trembled in her hand, and through the tear on her
lashes she saw Titania standing upon it in all her misty
and jewelled glory. The queen pointed to two flowers
lying out on the ground—one a deep, full rose, red as
a man's blood, and the other a pallid lily, shining like
a silver chalice in the rays of the moon.

" Here," said she, " is my gift ; the rose is Life, the
lily is Death ; choose which shall be placed in the
Baby's hand, for either is a priceless boon."

While she yet spoke a cloud passed over the moon,
and when the light shone out again the fairy court had
vanished, and the Poor Relation found herself alone,
the five-leaved clover withered in her hand, and at her
feet the Rose of Life and the Lily of Death.

All the rest of the night she could not sleep for
weighing in her mind which of the fairy's gifts she
should place in the Baby's hand, for she desired to do
only that which she thought would be most likely to
secure the child's true good. Life, with all the fairies
had bestowed, might be beautiful and brilliant, but
none of them had given a talisman to shield from

sorrow. She thought of her own sad years, and how often she had wished she had died when she was a baby, and so escaped the sin and trouble of existence. She thought, if the Baby died now, innocent and pure, it would go straight to heaven, and be a bright angel among God's cherubs, never to know the want and care, and pain of humanity.

But then this Baby had so much to live for—hope and friends, fame and fortune, and perhaps, who could tell? even happiness, for all hearts did not always suffer. So she could not decide; and when she arose she asked her white-haired old father as he sat in the sun on the porch:

"Which would be the best gift for a new-born babe, life or death?"

He looked curiously at her with his dim eyes, and answered:

"It is a hard question, for life is full of snares and evil, and when the babe has lived as long as I have it will know that all the hopes of life are not so sweet as the hope of death's long rest!"

And she asked the wrinkled mother who sat beside him, clinking the shining needles through the snowy wool; and the withered hands stopped their busy knitting for an instant as she said:

"Life is labor, but in the world after death we will neither toil nor spin!"

So she said to herself. "The old, for whom time is over, believe that death is a greater blessing than life. The old are wise; but they are also weary. Let me ask the young."

So she went into the house where the Crippled Sister was propped up on a couch by the window, weaving arabesque figures into a fine linen garment that swept down over her like a shroud; and she asked her also:

"Sister, which would be the best gift for a new-born babe, life or death?"

"Oh! life! life, of course!"

"But, Sister, there is so much pain in life—you and I know that?"

"Yes," replied the cripple thoughtfully; "but there is the air, the sun, and the flowers; the blue sky and the stars; the thought of God, and the joy of being!"

Then the Poor Relation smoothed the pillows behind her sister's crooked back, and went forth, saying softly, "Life is always hope to the warm blood of youth, for youth is not yet tired of woe and work." Then she concluded that the Baby should choose for itself; she would hold the two flowers over it while asleep, and whichever one its eyes turned upon when they first opened she would know was its destined fate. As she walked back over the field, where she had found the five-leaved clover the day before, the birds sang, the daisies nodded in the breeze, the lowing of kine reached her ears, and on the side of the purple hills a little way off she saw a bright stream leaping and flashing in the morning light. All things spoke of life, and that life was pleasant and fair. But as she went on farther she came to the still Churchyard, and looked in at the open gate. There lay the green graves with their white stones at the head and foot; the weeping willows drooping their graceful branches over the forgotten names; and all seemed so calm and holy, as if the sleepers there had folded their hands and lain down with the hush of prayer in their hearts; so that if life looked fair, death at least was peace. Still she mused, as she kept on her way, till she entered the quiet chamber where Baby slumbered in its warm nest. The room was darkened, for the pale Young Mother was asleep also; and the Fat Nurse was down-stairs in the kitchen, making her face redder than ever under her frilled cap as she stirred a saucepan over the hot fire, keeping her dignity while the cross cook fidgeted with the tongs. The Poor Relation leaned over the crib, holding in either hand the Rose of Life and the Lily of Death, and waiting for the Baby to open its eyes upon destiny. The tiny creature did not stir, but slept on till she began to tremble at the power she held, and to think she would carry both the flowers away and bury them in the garden at home. Then she feared the fairy might be angry, and send something worse than life or death upon the child as a punishment for the neglect of her gifts. Suddenly she bethought herself of the five-leaved clover, which she had hidden in her bosom; so she passed the two blossoms into one hand as she drew forth the faded charm, scarcely believing that the fairies could appear by day, or that the shrivelled plant kept its potency as a spell. But as she held it up Titania appeared, alone and mistier than ever, perched among the airy lace-curtains on the foot-board of Baby's bed.

"O Queen!" she cried, "bestow thine own gifts!

A mortal has not wisdom enough to decide a human fate!"

The queen smiled on her, and her crown of minute gems sparkled more brightly as she said:

" Didst thou not know that to find a five-leaved clover and to talk with fairies was to mark thee for trial of soul? Dost hesitate between my gifts, because sorrow comes into all life? Sorrow is life's discipline—an angel that leads immortals to loftier grace, and they stand higher in the next world who have suffered in this than they who have died unpained. Give this Baby life, for we, the fairies, have given her gifts that shall make her a glory on earth, and her life shall be example. But because we dare to yield naught that can ward off sorrow, I, Titania, will bestow upon her that which will make sorrow sweet, and stay with her as a joy stronger than despair, and a light in every darkness. She shall have Love—love from her birth and beyond her tomb; for Life with Love is richer than Death and Peace!"

And the fairy touched the lily with her sceptre, and she and it vanished away.

When the Young Mother woke she marvelled much

to see a beautiful crimson rose lying in the Baby's hand. The Baby too awoke, and looked at it, and smiled at the strange plaything. And because it was the first flower her child ever saw, because it came there in so wonderful a way, for even the Fat Nurse knew not who brought it, the Mother took it and pressed it in her Bible. And long after, when the Baby had grown up to be a lovely and noble maiden, worshipped and loved, humble and pure, and a blessing to the Poor Relation, she found it there, the mystic Rose of Life among the words of Christ.

II.

THE young Aunties had said it was a " rose-bud; " and when it woke from its noonday nap in its little white crib, it was a very blooming little bud indeed; its round dimpled face was pink with the warm flush of sleep ; its tiny lips, that had been softly sucking in a dream, were dewy and red as two unfolding leaves; its small, doubled fists, that it looked at so curiously with its wide blue eyes, were tinted in the tender palms like the satiny inside petals of a flower; and the wee balls of feet, that had kicked themselves out of their pretty socks, had such rosy soles, and such mites of cunning pink toes that the delighted Aunties might have thought each one was verily a sweet and separate blossom.

And it lay on its downy bed just like a bird in its nest, and cooed at its funny dots of hands, till the young Father and Mother, who had been sitting very quietly while Baby slept, hardly venturing to speak above a whisper for fear of stirring that sacred slumber, smiled at each other as they listened to that little chirp, and went side by side and leaned together over their treasure—God's crowning gift to holy human love.

They looked down on Baby with such shining faces that Baby left off studying its fingers, and looked up at them, with its bright bit of a dawning laugh, that made the admiring Mother lift it in her loving arms for the happy Father to kiss its damask cheek. And then they sat down to watch and wonder at the growing meaning in its ways; and while, with a solemn tenderness, they talked of what might be in the dim far-off of Baby's future years, there came a peculiar knock at the chamber door, vigorous and muffled, as if given by strong knuckles well-cased in folded flesh; and directly there entered in, puffing and beaming, the Fat Nurse in whose ample lap Baby had received its first notions of active life, when habitual trotting churned its daily bread into buttermilk. Instead of the frilled caps that had nodded over Baby's naps, she wore a large black bon-

2

net like a bombazine coal-scuttle, with an expansive
bow tied just in the crease of her double chin, and carried in one hand a swelling basket whose lid was intri-
cately fastened with a green ribbon, and in the other a
bulging cotton umbrella, stout in the stick and faded
in the stuff. She announced that having just finished
up one engagement, and being on her way to another,
she had dropped in to see how her former patients
were getting along ; and then carefully depositing basket and umbrella upon a chair, she loosened the bonnet
bow, flung the flowing strings over her broad shoulders,
and took the Baby right into her pillowy arms, as if,
while she was about, its place was only there. The
Mother saw that she looked at the infant with critical
eyes, and anxiously awaited her first remark. Gradually the long embroidered robe began to wave up and
down as the two cushioned knees fell into their usual
motion, and Baby's dinner kept time to the rolling,
mellow voice. " It's a growin' fust rate, mum ; it's as
fine a child as I've seed since I went a-nussin' ; my babies
mostly is good speciments ; it ain't got no marks nor dis-
torts, and no rashes nor chafes. You've did better than
most beginners with the fust ; it's pooty well over the

colic time, and ain't got a croupy neck, so I reckon it'll get on now all right."

The fair little Mother sparkled all over at the praise of Experience.

"Now, mum," Nurse continued, glaring benignly at the white robe that heaved up and down upon her spacious lap, "you haven't told me the young un's name?"

"Oh, Nurse," was the reply, "it's only ' Baby ' yet; we have hardly thought of any other name!"

"Well, now, that's uncommon," rejoined the Nurse in a meditative tone. "If it was the last of a beggar's dozen I could understand that you might have run out of names; but mostly there's one cut and dried for the fust afore it's born, and it pops into the world and its name both at onct."

"Yes," answered the Mother, "it is generally so; but there are so many to name our Baby after that it is hard to decide; we cannot name it for one of the Grandmothers without hurting the feelings. of the other; and if we were to call it after any of the Aunties, all the rest would think they were each neglected; and I do not wish it christened after me because it would seem so selfish, and there are so many pretty fancy names that we never know which to choose."

Nurse slowly laid again behind her broad back the bonnet ribbon that had dandled forward by degrees, and nodded assentingly to these confidential remarks.

"It's curious about names," she said. "I've been a-noticin' all my life that people grow like their names; Johns and Jameses ain't near so like to go to the bad as your Howards and Augustuses; for you see, fine names sort o' give young uns hifalutin' notions. Many a one I've seed onsettled, tryin' to match his doin's to a big-soundin' name, that might have turned out sober chap enough if them he belonged to had had sense to call him after some of the plain old Bible folk. Now there's me! You'd never guess what a name I've got; it was a sore point to me many a long year before I plucked up courage to put it down. My mother had been a-readin' some trash or other of a novel just afore I was born, and nothin' must do but I must be named after the young woman it was all about. So when daddy came into the room to see her and me, just as soon as she could gasp she ups and says, "It's to be Sophronisber, Bill; I've settled it so in my own mind.

The old man like to have gone off. 'Don't you think Susan would suit us better?' says he. 'Susan!' says she, a-turnin' up her nose, 'I ain't a-goin to have a child of mine called Susan!" 'And I don't think I can stand one of mine named Sofynisby! Lord, what a name!' says he. And so they bandied the two names, until mother she was a-gettin' excited and the old man mad; and Mrs. Jane Spotts, who was a-nussin' of her, she just took him by the collar and pulled him out of the room. But the long and the short of it is he wouldn't give in and neither would she, and so they tacked the two together, and there I was, Sophronisber Susan Boggers! And such a time as I had with that name! When I got big enough, the older children they all made fun of it, and plagued me half to death about it; and mother, she never called me nothin' but full Sophronisber, and dad, he never called me nothin' but Sukey, and it was 'Phrony,' and 'Sophy,' and 'Nis,' and 'Sue,' till I had as many names as a cat has lives. And after I grew up it got worse, till I was 'shamed as could be of the horrid sound, and ready to cuss my sponsors in baptism; the young fellows they sniggered over it, and the gals they just purtended they couldn't

say it, it was so long, and used to ask me to spell it for
'em, till I got so touchy over it it was a-spilin' my tem-
per, 'cause I wasn't born a vixen at all. But Howbe
ever, when Cuddle came along, and him and me was to
make a match, says he, " I don't like your name of Sophronisber!' 'No more do I,' says I. 'Let's drop it
then,' says he. 'Agreed,' says I. So we got the par-
son to say ' *Susan*, will you take this man ?' and made
him leave out the Sophronisber, and Mrs. Susan Cuddle
I have been ever since.   And so I never advise nobody
to stick a name to a child that 'll be a thorn in their
side, when more like most of 'em will have to be about
homely things than livin' like grand folks in a play.
How would it sound for me to be goin' out a-nussin'
and Bein' called 'Mrs. Sophronisber Cuddle'? You
ladies would think I was too fine to know my bizness.
No indeed!   Plain Susan for me, I say !"

Mrs. Cuddle's garrulous recital might have run on
interminably, to such polite listeners ; but while they
were laughing over it, the door opened, and in walked
quite a family procession bearing cautiously in their
midst a snowy box bound and tied up with bright and
dainty ribbons.   There were the Grandfathers leaning

sturdily on their gold-headed canes; and the Grandmothers in their shining black silks with their good-
natured faces just tipped to ruddiness by the outside
air; and the Young Aunties, a whole troop of them,
fresh and gushing and gay; and the Poor Relation,
clad in quiet dress, with the spiritual beauty of an un-
selfish life written on her countenance. And the blithe
and jubilant greetings all over, the Grandmothers laid
the box upon the bed, and with deft fingers undid the
fastenings and removed the lid, and lo! before all the
sparkling and admiring eyes, the wonderfully worked
and delicate, long christening robe! And because all
those who came with it had had some share in it, they had
made up this party to bring it all together to the only
Baby in the family on whom they all already doted.
One Grandfather had given the material; and the other,
who was something of an artist, in his leisure hours had
drawn the design, with quite a pride in its leaves and
flowers as they grew and entwined beneath his gold-
rimmed spectacles; and one Grandmother had made it
up, and the other had set in the lace-like wheels of some
fine old-fashioned stitch that had been familiar in the
far-off days of her girlhood; and the Young Aunties

had each embroidered buds and sprays, roses and scrolls,
with much comparing of work, and chatting over the
"Angel" who was to wear it; while the Poor Relation
had aided her Crippled Sister to finish it off with all
those parts which had required unwearying patience
and a steady hand. As it lay there before them, beautiful in feminine sight, a dumb, exquisite thing of cambric and thread, it seemed almost hallowed to the
mother's heart by reason of the richness of love that
had made it, and spoke to her, like a voice, of the tenderness with which old and young had wrought out
their thought for her little one; tears filled her soft
eyes; she reverently lifted the little dress and kissed it.
"O Baby!" she cried, with a sweet quiver in her
tones, holding it up before the unconscious optics that
were engaged in watching the bobbing up and down
of its other sweeping garments which the Fat Nurse
still monotonously kept going, "look what they have
done for you!   All of them, my darling, all of them!"
And then she laid the snowy robe carefully back on
the bed, and catching one head after another in her
embracing arms, caressed and thanked them, half laughing and half crying.   All talked at once, till an excited

Grandfather rapped upon the floor with his gold-headed cane, producing a moment's lull, of which he availed himself to speak.

" Here," said he, " is the christening frock ; but we have not heard yet what is the Baby's name ? "

And the Young Mother was again obliged to make humiliating confession that Baby was still a nameless waif ; whereupon arose once more a chorus of voices, exclaiming and suggesting, until the other Grandfather also called the meeting to order, and there was a general subsidence into a semicircle of chairs to debate the important question. The Young Mother took her Baby in her own arms, and sat upon the low seat in their midst, and the Father stood half behind her, looking down upon the two who were dearer to him than all the rest of the world, and it was the old, old picture of the Holy Family—the picture that stirred the hearts of dead and famous painters, till the most beautiful thing that art and religion and human spirits knew was this familiar vision of the mother and child ; for whether it be Mary and the infant Christ, or whether it be a modern mother and her baby, it is the highest and purest and loveliest picture that shines

2*

upon the dark backgrounds of life, and is seen in homes all over earth—the rich man's palace and the poor man's hut.

"Now, then," remarked Grandfather No. One, "the matter under discussion is, 'What is to be the Baby's Name?'"

"It appears to me," said Grandfather No. Two, "that this is not our business at all; it belongs to them," and he pointed with his cane to the Young Father and Mother.

"Well, now," chirruped Grandmother No. One, "it will be pleasant to talk it over, and if they have not made a choice, perhaps we can help them to something that will suit."

"Dear me!" exclaimed Grandmother No. Two, "it is a girl; and if a girl is pretty and nice, as our Baby is sure to be, it doesn't matter much what her name is!"

"Oh, don't it?" interposed the Fat Nurse, *sotto voce*, and the young couple smiled at the recollection of Mrs. Cuddle's early woes with her romantic cognomen.

"Call it after Sis," hypocritically observed one Young Auntie, indicating another Young Auntie with a slight flirt of her neatly-gloved hand.

" Oh, not for the world ! " impressively replied the other young lady; " *your* name is *so* much sweeter than mine that I am sure it ought to be called after *you !* "

And another Young Auntie sentimentally murmured, " Name it Angelina, do; because it is such a seraph, you know ! " And the Fat Nurse looked at her quench- ingly, and said so lugubriously, " Better Susan than Sophronisber ! " that they all laughed, though only Baby's Father and Mother understood the personal allusion.

And then, one after another, each proposed a differ- ent name, and the Young Mother had to exercise great tact and diplomacy to decline all without giving offence; and ever and anon she glanced over at the Poor Relation, who alone sat silent, gazing with floating eyes at the Baby and its parents, as if she saw the pic- ture Raphael painted, as if she comprehended the holi- ness of the child, the sanctity of the mother—she who would never have a baby of her own.

And they brought up all the family names, and those of Biblical heroines, from Eve to Phebe, whom Paul commended as a " succorer of many; " and there was much chiding of each other's tastes, and quips and quirks and merry sayings over the associations aroused, and affected little shrieks of horror from the Aunties at the unpoetic title of some otherwise forgotten ancestress, and much consequent recalling of family history, and great rolling of the eyes and raising of the hands at the Judiths and Deborahs of the Scriptures. But the young parents seemed hard to please, and objections were offered to everything proposed.

At last, one of the Grandmothers, who had had her ups and downs in life, and was therefore a rather worldly old lady in so far as she was anxious to save all those belonging to her from corresponding downs, and equally desirous to secure for them all possible ups, insisted upon a moment's silence of the mingling voices, as she had an important motion to make.

"My Dear," she said to the Mother, evidently considering the Father's opinion on the subject quite a secondary and insignificant consideration, "in naming the Baby would it not be well to regard something else than a mere pleasing of the fancy—your child's future advantage, for instance? Now, there's your Aunt Hannah"—here there was a simultaneous outcry from the

Aunties, which caused the Grandmother to shake her politic old head at them, and address the conclusion of her remarks to those fastidious butterflies. " Oh, yes! you midges," she continued, " I know it is not a pretty name; but Aunt Hannah is enormously rich, and has no one in particular to bequeath her money to, and never tells any one what she is going to do with it. .. She is a lone creature, and who knows but it would give her a new interest to have our little one called after her ; she might be enough pleased to make it her heir, and the very least she could do for the compliment would be to leave it a handsome sum for its name! " and the worldly old lady looked triumphantly around her as if she had unquestionably propounded a final satisfactory solution to the difficulty. There was a momentary pause ; even the most thoughtless and gushing of the Aunties saw the possible good thing for the Baby in the proposed arrangement, and had not the heart to venture a word against the chance of a prospective fortune for the general darling ; while the elder people waited in evident anxiety for the parents' reply, and Baby crowed away in happy unconsciousness of scheming sapience. But the Young Father's face flushed,

and the Young Mother lifted her graceful head a little
haughtily, as she emphatically answered :

"No, mamma, I will not lay upon my child's clean
life the stain of mercenary motive ! Not for all Aunt
Hannah owns would I have my Baby grow up to know
I had been so mean as to use its precious name as a
bait to catch money ! How could I teach her higher
things when she had learned 1 thought so much of
gold ? I could never look Aunt Hannah straight in the
face again ; I should be sure of her suspicion of design,
and I should feel as if I had given over Baby and myself to a degrading bondage of expectation depending
on another's death ! I will trust her good fortune to
God ; we must not stoop for it ! "

Grandfather No. One rapped approval with his gold-
headed cane and ejaculated, "Spoken like my own
brave lass ! " Grandfather No. Two said, with just a
perceptible inflection of disappointment, "When she
comes to our age she will have found out that money
is more useful than pride ! " The relieved Young
Aunties clapped their applauding hands, and the husband leaned over and kissed the delicate cheek, a trifle
paler from the unusual act of self-assertion against

maternal guidance, while the defeated Grandmother rustled her shining black silk, and grew rather redder in her ruddy face, as she somewhat testily exclaimed, " Well then, what *are* you going to name the child for, and *who* are you going to call it after ? "

A soft blush suffused the Young Mother's tender face, that had bent over her cooing Baby, and her voice took even a sweeter melody as she replied :

" Since we have been talking it over, quite a new thought has come to me about Baby's name. Nurse says that people grow like their names, but I myself have observed that children, in time, resemble the persons they are called for ; I suppose they naturally feel a peculiar interest in and try to imitate those whose name they bear ; and there is one we know whom I should like my little girl to model after, one who is good, and pure, and true ; who has kept a white soul through dark days and hard times ; who has been faithful in all things, thinking more of others than of herself ; never faltering in the path of right, and more nobly fearless before a wrong than any man I ever saw ; who is a ministering spirit to us all, and worthy of the best we can give her ; who lives humbly among

men, but never forgets the presence of her God!"
And the Young Mother rose up with her Baby in her
arms, and stood before the Poor Relation. "And so,
dear Cousin Mary," she said, "because I would have
my child grow like you, will you let me give her *your*
name?"

And the Poor Relation was so surprised and overcome at being thus honored in the midst of them all,
that she could scarcely speak; and the Father warmly
seconded his wife's requests, and the rest crowded
quickly around her, shook her hands, and made her
feel they were glad of the choice; for somehow the
Young Mother's little speech had suddenly set her before them in clearer light than they were used to see
her, and the beauty of her unobtrusive life glorified
her for a moment even more than the accepted fact
that she was henceforth an important member of the
family, since the first grandchild had been named after
her. And the worldly old Grandmother forgot the ups
and downs of the past and future, and magnanimously
said to her: "My daughter is wiser in her generation
than I; it *is* better to be good than wealthy;" while
the Fat Nurse, having sat the whole visit through, in

order to satisfy her curiosity as to what would be the end of it, tied her bonnet-strings in the crease of her double chin, picked up the portly basket and stout umbrella, ejaculating, " It's a heap more sensible then toadyin' rich folks in the cradle ! " and trotted off with very much the same motion as that which shook up so many infantile breakfasts. And then the family meeting broke up, wending their way in groups, talking it over still as they went.

As the Poor Relation walked homeward, there was a shining in her eyes, a color in her cheeks, and a lightness in her step, that had not been there for many a day ; the sun was brighter to her, the skies bluer, the fields greener, than she had ever seen them since her vanished youth ; she was full of yearning thoughts of the little one and its mother ; she even said over her own name to herself with a little happy laugh that was half a sob of delight too ; and she paused once to lift up her soul in an earnest, aspiring prayer that her Father in heaven would help her to keep her name worthy to be worn by the pure spirit whose angel beheld His face. She felt as if she had a partnership in this new being forever ; it was a fresh and solemn link to life and eternity. A rush of love for it flooded her heart, and she, who had neither husband nor child, understood for a moment the blissful sense of motherhood. But when she reached the vine-wreathed porch where her Aged Father and Mother sat together in the declining golden sun, she sank down on the steps at their feet, and could only cry like a very touched and tender woman, as she told in her sweet and simple way about this Naming of the Baby.

III.

EVERYBODY said that there never was such a Baby; and being the first one for many years in two very large families, there were plenty of voices to ring perpetual changes of admiration on its growing beauties and graces; especially were the Young Aunties—that gay and gushing troop of happy girls, enthusiastic over the little treasure of human life that made such funny passes at their bright ribbons with its tiny dots of hands, or crowed with delight in answer to their unwearied efforts at entertainment. Never did any other baby born into this world possess such lovely eyes, or such bewitching dimples, or such beautiful golden rings of hair! The flesh of all infants is soft, but surely none other ever had such a pure and velvety skin! And oh, the little pink-soled feet! was there ever anything on earth so cunning and so tender as

those plump, helpless activities tipped with such minute and perfect bits of toes ?   Then the intelligence of
this precious pet !   How they chronicled among themselves its dawning smiles, and its pin-provoked percep-
tions of pain—symbol of many another torture that life
endures from unperceived moral pin-pricks.   How
they saw intellect written on its expanding brow, and
detected offered kisses in the dewy mouth pouting with
undissipated dream of milky draught!   And the like-
nesses they perceived, even in the scarcely defined nose
and decidedly double chin !   And the predictions they
made of romantic destinies in the future, and the
delight and wonder and half-motherliness they all had
over this live doll, that somehow stirred up the woman-
hearts of these untried natures into vague longings and
instinctive sympathies!   Every morning, when the
Young Mother went through her greatest enjoyment of
giving her Baby its daily bath with her own hands,
there was sure also to be a fair and smiling Auntie
beside the little tub to sing or chirrup down the faint,
gasping cry at the first plunge in the clear water, to
plash with rosy fingers the warm, lucid drops over the
fat and dimpled shoulders, or to watch with dancing

eyes the round, white limbs kicking up the shining waves against the soft, bare body, and the Baby would crow up to the Young Mother and the Young Auntie, and they would chorus the crow, and laugh back together in so sweet and innocent happiness, and talk broken English to their darling both at once, till it was better than any play to see, and a sort of unwritten poem of the pure joy of humanity.

And never was a Baby that had apparently as many needs as this one; never were a deft set of Aunties so busy in providing superfluities of worsted and embroidery; patterns became their chief interest, and new designs their perpetual quest; knitting-needles clicked constantly, and coquettish crochet-baskets hung gracefully from the silken belts; and the result was that Baby had socks enough for a centipede, small blankets sufficient to clothe a moderate-sized tribe of Afghans, more bibs than would protect the undeveloped necks of an orphan asylum, and sacks and caps and wraps of all shapes and materials enough to have fitted out half a dozen destitute missionary boxes; and in fact the perplexed Young Mother did surreptitiously bestow upon less favored infancy many a donation from the overflowing wardrobe of this fortunate mite. But the generous Young Aunties did not miss anything; they had time and zephyrs in plenty, love and leisure in full; so they went on industriously increasing the store, and glowing over their own good works.

Once, on a sunny morning, one of the brighest, and gayest, and cheeriest of the Young Aunties set out for the Baby's home with another new gift for the precious little one—a light, white, dainty thing, fleecy as a cloud and warm as the eider-duck's down. She did not step out quite as briskly or into as springy a walk as the Young Aunties generally were wont to do, for there was an air of expectancy in the lingering pace, and a sort of watchful, yet timid hope in the lustrous hazel eyes, which betokened that some one could gladden the sight thereof. But suddenly the walk quickened a little, and the white lids dropped their curled lashes upon the flushing cheek, as a tall figure hove in view with an unmistakable sea-roll in the gait, and then there was a greeting, half-cordial and half-shy, and the handsome Young Sailor turned about and walked on with the Young Auntie. Suddenly for those two—chatting lightly of this thing and that, of the weather at home and on the ocean waves, of the last party and the latest news, even of the Baby in their blithe and blissful mood—for those two all the common way before them was changed to a golden street; the soft air intoxicated them with gladness, and the sunshine seemed to fold round them warm and bright, as if to shut out all the rest of the world, and life was beautiful on the happy earth as in those ancient days of innocence and Eden, for they were young, they were together, and their hearts were trembling with the joy of a yet unspoken dream. For this gallant officer, who had more than once faced death undaunted by danger, and undismayed by stormy winds of tempest or of battle, had never found courage to speak three little words to the fair girl whom he loved better than his life. And she, oh! be sure, she was gay and gleeful with him, and believed she gave no sign of the sweet secret that tinted her soft cheeks whenever he drew near, and filled the sparkling eyes with such new and tender light. At last they reached the Baby's home, and he was loth to leave her, and she longed for him to linger; so upon half a hint she breathed an invitation, that seemed like a blessing, for him to come into the

house and wait till she had given the Baby her gift,
and then—oh, then they both knew ·there would be
another walk back upon the golden street !

But as the young man sat waiting in the quiet parlor
while the Young Auntie ran upstairs to caress the Baby
and present the last marvellous effort in zephyrs, he saw
her still before him ; it seemed to him that he should
always see her as he had looked upon her that morning
in her youth, and grace, and peerless beauty; that she
could never change or grow old to him, but would for
ever and ever live in his heart as fresh, as pure, as en-
chanting as to-day—his first true love, the one woman in
all the world for him. And after a mental spasm of
great humility as to his own unworthiness, and an inward reproof of his own presumption in aspiring to the
love of a being so angelic, there came into his mind a
nervous impatience of any longer delay in learning his
fate, and he determined that, come what would, he
would ask her to be his before they parted again that
day; but how to do it, oh! how to do it? That was the
question he was revolving in uneasy perplexity, when,
pit-a-pat, he caught the tapping sound of her tiny, high-
heeled boots, and his heart leaped as she stood before

him again. Was it a mere artifice of feminine coquetry, or was it some deeper womanly instinct, that had made her throw off her hat and bring down the Baby in her girlish arms to show the embarrassed Young Sailor the Family Pride, of whose infantile perfections he had heard so much from the adoring Aunties? And the Baby cooed, and the Young Auntie chirruped, bending her bright face over the downy little head that nestled against her bosom; and a new vision flashed into the lover's dream—the sweet vision of wife and child upon hearthstone of his own—the first vague, longing sense of fatherhood inherent in man's nature awoke at the recognition of the intuitive motherliness in the woman's; it added a strong and tender yearning to the passionate love; it calmed the unquiet of his doubts, and steadied his trembling purpose, as with almost conscious ownership he leaned over the Baby and its bonny nurse.

"Just listen to its darling baby-talk!" cried she, delighted with Baby's amiability in showing off. "Oh, you precious petty, coo—coo—coo!"

"Coo—coo—coo!" gurgled back the echoing tones from the little dot of a rosy mouth.

3

"Do you understand that sort of language?" quietly the bold Young Sailor asked.   •

"Of course," was the indignant reply; "everybody that has anything to do with a baby knows just what it means; there, it is coo-cooing now to tell you it understands all you say!"

"Then, Baby," he gravely said, and somehow he caught the tiny ball of a fist and the young girl's little white hand both at once in his big brown one, "tell your dear Auntie how truly I love her, and how much I hope to call her mine!"

It was all done, and the Young Auntie never knew what she answered, or how it came to pass; but she and Baby were gathered up together in the strong arms, and half-laughing, half-crying, she soothed the Baby's astonished cry between the first kisses of first love. When the Young Mother heard the faint echo of that sudden, sharp wail, she sped unsuspectingly down-stairs to see what was happening to her child; and, as she floated into the room, she read the old, old story that was being told over again with her Baby in the midst thereof—her Baby, that was now gazing up with wise, wide eyes into the Young Auntie's blushing countenance, and was so

encircled by two pairs of arms that she scarcely knew
which to take it from; but after a loving embrace and
a hearty hand-shake, she carried Baby off at last, recalling her own cherished love-tale, and left the happy
young lovers to themselves.

Soon after this there was a gay wedding, with a long
train of the other Young Aunties for bridesmaids, and
a grand show of uniforms, and a bright glancing of
naval buttons that made Baby's eyes dance with delight,
for Baby was particularly and pressingly invited to the
marriage; and when the gray-haired minister solemnly
asked, "Who giveth this woman to be married to this
man?" cooed out so loud and so long that a general
smile burst out among the audience, and even made
rainbows in the Grandmother's glistening tears.

Then, in a little while, there was one of those sad
partings that wring the life from out young hearts, and
a gallant ship had gone to sea, while a fair bride was
left at home to count the days of absence.

Then came watchings for interminable letters, anxious suspense over a single missing mail, shudders at
news of storms and disasters on the ocean, and a gradual
sedateness, growing from an absorbing interest, settling

the gushing gayety of girlhood. Then there was an
unusual silence; more than one appointed time passed
away and brought no letter; a frightened, far-off look
clouded the old brightness of sparkling eyes, and even
the postman hurried with averted head more swiftly
by the wistful face watching him from the window,
knowing well that among the many messages he carried of love and life and death, there was none for
her. And then at last there was published the awful
news that thrilled the land—the ship he sailed in had
gone down at sea, and every soul on board had
perished.

The worst anguish of life had fallen on her—such
agony as comes but once to a woman, and pales forever
the storied tortures of the Burning Lake; that takes all
values out of the things of this world, in which eternity
becomes comprehensible through the infinitude of
suffering, and the terrible solitude of the spirit which
for the time is reached and touched by nought in the
universe, neither God nor man. She sat in the midst
of mourning friends, but shed no tear; all the great
salt- waves of the unfathomed ocean were sweeping
over him; tears of hers could not even fall upon his

grave; words of tenderness, of consolation, of hope
beyond the tomb, were spoken to her; she heard only
the moaning sound of the never silent sea; day and
night, in her thoughts and in her dreams, she saw a ship
go down into the deep, and beheld the cruel and
hungry waters sweeping over the swaying form of her
dead. She sat in darkness, for the light of day was
a mockery; she rose up and lay down as she was
directed, but she neither spoke nor noticed any living
being save the gentle Poor Relation, whose mission
on earth seemed to be that of ministering to those sick
and in affliction; she appeared to have a dim perception, born of that insight into another's grief that
personal endurance sometimes gives, that here too was
a lonely soul that had suffered loss and known sorrow's
worst extreme, and in a mute, pathetic fashion she
clung to her a little, following her movements with
her listless glance, and laying her weary head upon the
patient breast. One day, the old family doctor, who
had held her in his arms when she had uttered life's
first gasping cry, came from her room with a troubled
face, saying softly in tremulous tones, "She must weep,
or she will die." And they gathered about her—all

those she most loved—the Mother and the Father and all the saddened Young Aunties, and talked, tenderly before her of her lost husband; praised his beauty and his ways, his courage and his worth, and raised up their voices and wept for him in her presence. She rocked herself back and forth, and moaned as they spoke, but she listened with dry eyes still, and a touching terror pervaded the hushed household.

But one day, when the Poor Relation necessarily returned to her own home, she entered the chamber where her Crippled Sister, with tireless fingers, wove embroidered flowers into fine, flowing muslin, and lo! she was softly keeping time to the leaf-forming stitches with the plaintive rhythm of Tennyson's sweet song, "Home they brought her warrior dead." Oh, what a thought flashed into the Poor Relation's mind! Out of the house she flew like a bird, and with swift feet fled along the way that had been to the lovers a golden street, and breathless, entered the nursery where Baby slept the rosy sleep of innocence.

A few explanatory words to the sympathetic Young Mother, pale also with sisterly anxiety, and Baby was lifted out of its warm nest, fortified with requisite

refreshment, and wrapped in the very white and fluffy
thing that the Young Auntie had brought it on the
eventful morning of her love ; and then back with bur-
dened arms and swelling heart sped the Poor Relation
to the sorrow-stricken dwelling. She crossed the shad-
owed room unnoticed, and softly laid the little one on
the widowed breast. For the first time the pallid lips
quivered, and Baby—the blessed Baby—looked up into
the drawn and colorless face, and cooed and cooed as if
it had brought a message. Then, at the sweet, familiar
sound, the tears burst out, and flowed and flowed, and
great sobs shook her fragile frame, and the Poor Relation cried also, and the tears of the two women mingled
and fell fast like fountains upon the Baby, till Baby
began to feel very damp, and so joined in and took a
good cry too.

Every day after that the Poor Relation came on her
errand of mercy, bearing the Baby, whose unconscious
ministry was softening this stony grief; for wifehood
may pass away, widowhood may be overlived, but the
sense of motherhood that has been or might have been,
lies very deep in the heart of a woman. But one day,
as she entered the house, Baby was suddenly snatched

away from her, all the Young Aunties seemed to clutch
her at once, and half carried her into the presence of a
sunburned Sailor, who caught her in his strong embrace
as if she had been his own sister. And then was told
the wonderful story of the wreck, and the rescue by a
homeward-bound but slow-sailing vessel, and a chorus
of carefully toned voices repeated, "And now, Cousin
Mary, *you* must tell her, you must tell her right
away!"

Once more in the lonely and darkened chamber, the
Poor Relation put her arms around the pale girl-wife,
who wondered now why she had come without the
Baby.

"My darling, I have brought you something even
sweeter than the Baby," was the gentle answer; "a
very gospel, dear heart; good tidings of great joy."

"Joy to me, Cousin Mary? Oh, never again! The
awful sound of the sea shuts out all good tidings from
me forever."

"But, dear child," and the Poor Relation held her
very close to her own beating heart, "you know we are
told of a time when the sea shall give up its dead.
Sometimes, oh, sometimes, it is not only at the last day!

Ships go down, but other ships are on the waters, and oh, darling, darling, sailors are sometimes saved !"

Joy rarely kills. She rose quickly up, she pushed away the encircling embrace, a faint flush flashed into her wan face and a light into her eyes; she stretched her arms towards the door, she cried out, wild with a new hope, " Oh, Cousin Mary, he has come home, he has come home !"

The door flew open. There was a rush and a rapture of meeting like the bliss of heaven. The sea had given up its dead. And as the Poor Relation slipped out, the Mother kissed her in the entry, the Father shook both her hands upon the stairs, and all the Young Aunties hugged her and Baby alternately, for was it not her happy thought that had chased death and saved the sister for her husband ? And it was once more Baby who had given this woman to this man.

3*

IV.

BABY'S NURSE.

The Young Mother was in despair; Baby was no light weight, and her heart was heavy; her arms were tired, and her mind was worried; because for nearly two weeks the Young Mother had been Baby's only nurse. Not that all ministrations for her child were not sweet and holy as ever; not that Baby's little body was not more precious than fine gold; but the extra care and fatigue added to her other duties, the confinement to the house, the weariness of an imperative work which required attention to be constantly on the alert and yet left no trace of its exaction, was beginning to tell on her whole nature, of which the flesh was weaker than the willing spirit. For the Young Mother had had sad experiences of helps and hinderances in the shape of Nursemaids; she had come to consider Baby's life as a "brand snatched from the burning" of incompetency and ignorance, and, from the utter carelessness and un-motherliness of those who went about as accomplished handmaids, had almost been inclined to credit the doctrine of total depravity. So that she had grown cautions and particular in her selection of a new girl; and having conceived certain transcendental ideas that at the root of all service to humanity, whether from high or low, there must be Love as an inspirer and instigator of faithful duty, it was not very likely she would very soon find requisite fineness in the Hibernian material that generally applied for the situation, with a much stronger interest in wages and perquisites than in the labor and tenderness which was expected for them.

And if Baby could have spoken in any other language than a coo and a cry, what a tale the small creature could have unfolded of torments manifold and infantile endurance! of the brawny Celt who tossed the tiny form in the air, too frightened to make vocal protest, and who trotted her bony limbs persistently, kneading the sensitive flesh with bumps and bruises, and who vigorously stuck promiscuous pins through the soft raiment without the slightest regard to the position of the points; of the sly, sleek "professioner," who surrepti-

tiously administered paregoric that she might slip away
to the pious enjoyment of love-feasts with an admirer
who waited at the back gate; of the French bonne,
whose broken chatter banished sleep and whose sole
idea of infant needs was confined to a perambulator on
the most crowded streets; of the middle-aged familiar,
whose " sober and honest " character was attested by a
private bottle which proved detrimental to her charge
to the extent of sundry knocks and falls; and of the
half-grown assistance who ate up all the pap, and proclaimed aloud that " Baby was wisibly swellin' with too
much stuffin."

It seemed as if through the very innocence and help-
lessness of her Baby the Young Mother had first learned
the moral destitution, the lack of all sense of responsibility which leavens so much human nature with wickedness and vice; it made her heart-sick sometimes to
feel her trust in her fellow-creatures so rudely disturbed,
and to comprehend how much the lower strata of people required educating and elevating; yet, as she knew
from her own experience that men and women were
not all alike, and that the world held sweetest and best
as well as warped and worst, so she kept also her faith

that even in the hardest and basest there was something, if it could be got at, by which each might be lifted to a higher level; and as she pondered these things often in the pure charity of her soul, she had the strong longing of impressible spirits to instruct and uplift the ignorant and the evil; only in these individual cases her own environment proved too strong for her, and Baby's life, health, and comfort were too dear and too important to afford time and patience for experiment. So, with her instincts sharpened by fresh knowledge and maternal anxiety, she watched and waited for another servitor in whom feeling and fidelity should equal self-interest, and control the enmity cultivated towards employers. She grew too to understand that if her overflowing mother's love was not proof against the monotony and weariness of care-taking, it could hardly be considered an unmitigated privilege by a stranger to have the constant guardianship of the most angelic baby that ever breathed; and a great compassion fell upon her for those to whom labor, unlightened, by affection, is a necessity and a grievance.

So day after day went by, and as one after another candidate for the place was rejected, the sympathetic

Grandmothers, who had hopefully haunted Intelligence Offices, began to think she was too hard to suit, and were inclined to leave her to her own devices at last in the search. The hearty Grandfathers told her she was getting thin and pale with her impracticable fancies, and that she had better put up with any Bridget that came along, rather than wear out her youth and beauty in a hunt for the undiscoverable ; and even the Young Husband gently reproved her for supposing she could ever receive heart-work for hire. The Young Aunties fluttered in, turn about, with sisterly desire to help and relieve ; they each chirped and played a little while with delighted Baby, like the veriest bright and happy children, and while the novelty lasted Baby responded to their enthusiasm and entertainment with all gladness and gayety that called forth an unfailing ingenuity of pet names. But when Baby's attention was no longer to be cajoled with caressing tones or tapping on the window-panes ; when it came to the uninteresting task of holding for any length of time a growing and unmindful weight ; when there were unaccountable wails to be soothed, and distracting screams to be pacified or explained, then the Young Aunties felt that they had

mistaken their vocation, and looked so forlorn and
tired, and tried so hard to be patient, that the Young
Mother always made some excuse to release them, and
contrived to send them home without having their confidence entirely shaken in Baby's perfections. But the
Poor Relation came in occasionally when she could
spare time, and gladly gave the Young Mother some
little comfortable rest, while Baby nestled contentedly
in the willing arms that never wearied of well-doing,
and who, while she thus eased another's burden, forgot her own awhile, as, looking into the tiny face, she
dreamed many a dream of the might have been.

It was now one of those rare and lovely days, when
Summer, lingering long through the Autumn, brings
all that she can of light and heat and color to crown
her ensuing departure ; when the warmth was like
early June, and the sky a July heaven, while through
all the air was a soft and scarcely perceptible haze
which sheds upon the October world that indescribable
pensiveness which is not sadness, and yet which tem-
pers joy. And to indulge in this last spell of the season's sweetness, the Young Mother had brought Baby
to the open parlor window, who looked out in serene

quietude at opposite trees and passing sights. There was a solemn stillness in the atmosphere, such as sometimes comes with the changing of the leaves, as if nature waited in sweet expectancy of crimson and gold for the coming silence of the snows or the gathering storms of winter, and the whole circumstance of time and conditions touched and filled the gentle heart with yearning without pain which lies among those deep things of God which brings the divine into human life. As she sat there, holding her Baby in her arms, a woman came slowly along on the other side and paused before the window—a woman, haggard, jaded, dust-stained; young in years as the Young Mother, but with the flowers of youth withered on the pale cheeks and pallid mouth. An image of desolate dejection, she had moved on till Baby's face caught her aimless sight, and wild light flashed into her dreary eyes; she tossed up her arms and stood still, looking over with such hungry, wistful gaze as made her whole pitiful figure almost pathetic; then, as if involuntarily drawn by an irresistible attraction, she crossed the street and came close to the house. The Young Mother shrank just a little, for at the first moment she thought the poor creature was insane; but her innate delicacy prevented her from showing fear or aversion, and the mood of the day and season was still upon her; besides, such a thin, thin hand was laid upon the sill, and such a wan, eager countenance was lifted to her own, that her compassion welled up into words.

"What is it?" she said with such womanly sympathy in her voice that it was like balm to the wounded. "Are you sick, or in want? Can I help you?"

And the woman gave a short, gasping sob, and stretched out her hands to her. "Only let me kiss your baby!" she cried.

The Young Mother naturally hesitated, but the woman went on.

"Oh, it is so long since I have seen a baby! Ah, Madam! you are good, you are happy; you don't know sorrow; you don't know sin; you don't know what it is to have lost your baby and to go about the world with empty arms and despairing heart. Mine is gone—gone! but it seems to me if a baby's pure lips could but touch mine again, I would be more fit to die!"

With an intuition like an inspiration the Young Mother saw that this being had wronged her own womanhood, and had suffered through her motherhood; that the sin and the suffering had been too great for her to bear, and that she was about to take her life to end it all. An exceeding pity flashed the tears into her eyes; the sin shocked her, but the evident suffering and punishment atoned. She could not send away, perhaps to her death, another fellow-creature, if a word or deed of hers might stay her; a woman, poor, wan, and distressed, who wanted nothing but a baby's kiss, was surely worth saving; a woman who grieved for a dead baby must have that in her that a little child could lead; and perhaps the dear Father in Heaven had sent this fallen sister to her Baby for redemption! She paused a little space as these thoughts filled her mind— paused, looking down into the sad face, over which there gradually rose a deep flush of shame as the silence was misinterpreted into scorn; then the worn figure turned to go away with a fresh bitterness gathering in the heart. But the Young Mother leaned forward, and laid a hand on her shoulder. "Wait!" she said, and rose up from the window. She went to the door with her baby on her breast, passed down the steps, took the thin hand in her own, and led the surprised woman into

the house—into the house and upstairs to her own
chamber, placed her in her own low chair, and laid the
Baby in her arms. Bewildered by this unexpected
kindness, the woman sat silent; but when the soiled bonnet was gently removed, and a soft touch smoothed her
hair, she looked up into the sweet face bending over
her, and beheld there such a loving sympathy, that all
the flood-gates were opened, and she lifted up her heart
and wept—wept as the Young Mother had never seen
any one weep before, with the speechless agony of an
overcharged spirit, till at last the other, in the fulness
of compassion, put her arms about her and rested the
drooping head upon her pure bosom; and after a while,
when there came a peace after the tempest of tears, she
brought food and water, that cleansing and refreshing
might give strength and comfort; and when her strange
guest thanked her in broken tones, she said, tenderly
as one would touch a bleeding sore :

"Would you mind telling me your story? Maybe it
will give me some idea of how I can help you."

The woman wrung her hands. "Ah! you have been
so good, so good!" she cried. "Let me go, let me go!
There is no help for such as I! There is nothing left,

nothing, but to get out of the world! You have held
my head upon your breast, you have put your clean
arms about me, you have given your Baby into mine!
That is enough! You might be sorry, if you knew all
about me, that you ever touched or spoke to me! Oh,
let me go!"

But the Young Mother held her, and pleaded with
her, and bade her believe that her heart was not a
stone; that because of their mutual womanhood and
motherhood she could not let her go forth again without some effort to do her good; that they were alone
there with God and each other, and she might speak
freely, if thereby might come healing to her; that she
must not think of judgment and condemnation, but
only that she was bringing her sorrow to a sister and a
friend. Then the woman wept again, but tenderness
prevailed, and after a little she told all her miserable
tale—told it with tears and terrible effort—told it with
unaffected earnestness and simple pathos—told it as one
only tells a heart-history in the supreme crisis of an
unhappy life.

She was left an orphan when too young to remember
her parents, and had been taken in charge by some dis-

tant relatives who owned a large and lucrative farm. They were cold, selfish, puritanical people, with too much pride to let one of their own blood go to the poor-house—whose sole idea of child-training was filling the stomach and clothing the back, and who were only kind because they had no provocation to be otherwise, for this child grew to be sufficiently useful to earn all she received. She had been educated at the country school, where, having absorbed all there was to teach, she had learned, among other acquirements, to keep accounts and sew beautifully; so that she willingly acted as clerk and seamstress, and took her share in the lighter labors of her home. She looked after and loved the dumb creatures, with a friendliness the greater that she had not many human interests. The cows and horses knew her, the sheep came at her call, the poultry clustered round her, and the pigeons lighted on her shoulders; she made hay in the fields, picked wild flowers in the woods, berries by the brookside. Even her duties were light to her, because youth and health sets a glad heart singing at even the heaviest work; and altogether she lived a peaceful, happy, idyllic life, till womanhood imperceptibly dawned on her, ignorant

as a little child about everything except her own experience, and scarcely conscious that there was any larger
world beyond the limits of the farm.

Then came a day when one was thrown from his horse
in a roadside near by, and with much hurt carried into
the house, to be laid down for weeks of weariness and
pain ; he was left pretty much to her care and attend-
ance, for the elder people had too much to do—little patience with the delicate requirement of sickness and
refinement. Then came the long, bright summer hours
of convalescence, when, with books brought from the
city, he opened up a new world to the young girl sitting
at his feet, with upraised face all aglow, drinking in the
poetry of love and the poison of unconscious passion.
The young simplicity, the unworldly trust, the tender
face were fair and sweet to the ennuied man of the
world, and to the fickle sense gave the new attraction of
change from familiar interests. And so, not being entirely a fiend, without perhaps intending evil, he won
the unreasoning worship of an unconventional heart;
while her careless guardians noticed nothing, considering her still a child, after the fashion of those who do
not realize the growing years in others, and have no

particular intuition of affection to guide them to the truth.

At last the days and hours of his stay were numbered; time and occasion stirred the man's uncontrolled blood. Cunning words were spoken; practised eloquence bewitched; vows and promises were made—and how was this inexperienced girl to know the true from the false? All the centred and innate love, which had hitherto found so little response, was poured out like water from a pure fount. And she was so innocent—so innocent and untaught, and felt only that Love was sacred, and conceived of no evil that could come of it; cared only that she was his—his, body and soul, and rejoiced that she had all her life before her to think of and adore him. Only the bitter pain of parting stabbed her happy dream, and the days grew suddenly long and lonely, weighed upon her waiting spirit, buoyed up also with the sure hope that he would come again. She thought it was his continued absence, her morning expectation and nightly disappointment, the yearning wonder of unbroken trust that no word ever came to her, which made her step so heavy, her face so wan, and her work so tiresome and distasteful. She was so innocent—so innocent and igno-

rant that she comprehended neither her physical suffering, or even that she had sinned. Some interior sense
—not shame, but surprise and uneasiness—made her
hide herself from curious looks and significant glances,'
until, in her very innocence and ignorance, feeling as if
life was slipping away from her, and that she could not,
must not die till he came to her again, she must needs ask
relief from her pain. Then was opened upon her the tor-
rent of questions and reproach, scorn and knowledge, and
thus she learned that she had sinned and fallen, and was
no more fit to dwell with the virtuous and right-minded.
Confused and crushed, maddened by jibe and curse, she
fled away to the great city where he lived, to search for
him there, and find love, and rest, and justice. She had
little money and no friends, so she managed to get enough
needlework from the stores to give her sustenance while
she walked the streets week after week, looking into the
faces of the passers-by, always watching, always searching, for she knew naught of him but his name—and in
a large metropolis what is one man in the myriad of
rushing throngs? Up and down, back and forth, night
and day, in sunshine and in rain, in frost and snow she
went, with her wistful eyes and sinking soul; always

watching, always searching; keeping hope alive with his remembered words; clinging still to her faith in him, because she yet. knew so little of the world and humanity. Up and down, back and forth, after nights of tears and through days of anguish, in cold, and hunger, and bodily torment, till nature could hold out no more, and she fell fainting by the way, to be picked up as a cumberer of the streets and sent to one of those hospitals with which charity sanctifies the worst Babylon. Here her baby was born, and upon the darkness of her despairing desolation there fell the solemn and awful sweetness of a mother's love, that mighty and instinctive gush of tenderness with which a woman envelops the one thing which is indeed her very own.

But she would not linger, even for her child's sake; and with her infant in her arms, she sought work, and again commenced her weary search. Sometimes, when rare opportunity occurred, she asked for him; but as she came in contact with none of his order, she received no information; and once again she haunted the streets, always looking for the one face she never saw. But her baby comforted her. Like Correggio's Madonna, she knelt before it worshipping, felt as if an angel

4

dwelt with her; knew herself to be purified and forgiven in the divine eyes by the holiness of her motherhood, and her heart and hope waxed strong in her body
weakened by want and exposure. But one day, even
more restless than usual with her ever constant waiting,
she had gone abroad, up and down, back and forth,
watching and searching still, till she came upon a crowd
gathered about a church door, looking for a new-made
bride to come forth in the splendor of wealth and the
glory of beauty ; the wedding-bells rang gayly through
the clear air ; the merry group chatted and jested ; the
fine carriages blocked up the highway. She stood still,
as she did in all such musterings to gaze expectantly on
the faces around, never thinking of the couple that the
white-robed priest was blessing in the midst of a stately
company—a poor, sad, deserted mother, in a faded dress,
with a quiet baby in her arms. There was a stir, an
opening of doors, a rush of music, a flashing of diamonds and gleaming of white garments, and then over
the pealing of the bells, through the marriage march of
the organ, rose a terrible cry of murdered hope, as a
stricken woman fell insensible at the bridegroom's feet,
and the shrinking bride beheld a pale baby caught up

from the folds of her costly lace. Did he know her,
after those many months, so changed from the brightness and bloom of happy and glowing girlhood? Did
remorse, then and there, strike a sharp fang into his
conscience to sting with memory through all eternity?
Who knows? He made no sign. He led his wife
around the prostrate form, placed her in her carriage
with tender and assuring words, turned again and gave
money to a bystander for the unfortunate being who
had so unseasonably swooned, and then sank back upon
the satin cushions beside his bride, and was whirled
away to luxury and ease, honor and high place. And
the wedding-bells filled the air with their glad pealings,
the music of the organ rolled out from the magnificent
church, and humble hands lifted mother and babe out
of the way of the gay assembly which poured out from
that ceremony which had proclaimed before the altar
that God had joined together those two! She also
went her way from the church door, companied by
misery and uncomforted even by her child. She
wandered on, wandered on day and night, up and
down, back and forth, watching no longer, searching no
more, but as one stunned by a blow or walking in a

dream; her money gone—for she would take none of
his; too wretched to work, cast out and roofless in her
poverty; with the streets and houses, men and women,
trees and sky, all like shadows in a strange vision; even
the baby at her breast seemed unreal, like a phantom
carried in sleep, till its plaintive moans pierced to the
depths where maternity survived, though all else was
slain, and roused her to the bitterness and sharp agony
of reality. She begged for a pittance to preserve her
child; she grew frantic at the cries she could not still;
she clasped it close to her bosom to give it warmth;
she called out to the passers-by to look at her baby, to
tell her what was the matter with it—oh! what was the
matter with it? and what should she do? And some
stopped and did look, and shook their heads, and went
on, and some thought she was insane; and she knelt
down in the shades of evening on the cold stones, and
prayed and prayed to the Great Power that seemed so
far off, while His Angel Death stood so near by; and
then she gazed down at the little white face grown
suddenly still, and went wholly mad.

It was long past midnight, when a noisy group of
such women as only haunt the streets at such hours,

came laughing and capering out of a heated dance revel, singing their loose songs, and chaffing each other in that fictitious gayety born of wine and excitement; on they flung, a half-dozen reckless and ruined creatures, caring naught for man or heaven, with their mirth ringing hollow beneath the stars, and their peacock plumes mellowed by the moonlight; on they came to where a single figure stood upon the pavement, holding a dead baby in her arms, and babbling of brooks and fields. They paused, at first wondering at the burst of childish talk that greeted them, and then closed round about her in a ring of sad and pitying faces.

Perhaps it was the young visage, so wan and pathetic, that touched them; perhaps it was the dead baby that awed them; perhaps the dethroned mind that shocked them; or perhaps from their own experience they divined something of her unhappy story. Their levity died away, their quips and quirks were silenced, their bacchanal song was strangled by a sigh, their hearts and eyes filled up, and all that came out from them was pure, womanly in look, in voice, in deed. They took the small, cold form reverently out of the straining arms; with tender words and gentle caress they soothed the perturbed spirit, and lovingly and kindly as sisters led her to their own abiding place, and ministered to her in turn during a long and life-threatening illness, with the care, the patience, the generosity of closest kinship; and while she lay alike unconscious of good offices and personal grief, took her little infant and placed it solemnly, with church service of chant and scripture, in its grave within a suburban cemetery, shedding tears over the "earth to earth" that might have washed white many a sin and relieved more than one memory.

While she was sick and weak they were all forbearance and goodness towards her, but with the faint· bloom of returning strength their former indifference and carelessness came back, and they spake many a bitter truth, in their flippant way, of the world and men that subverted any dawning hope of·. help to be gathered therefrom ; and they shared with her freely and unsparingly, without counting the cost of their ill-gained gold. She had no other friends; in the whole wide world she had not one to go to for succor, for counsel, for upholding ; none cared for her save only these in a sort of fellowship of good-will; she was reck-less of herself, ruined as they were, with hell-fire in the past and an outlook of despair in the future. So she was fain to stay with them, to become one of them, to strive to drown in wild orgies the gnawing recollec-tions, to smother beneath the life of the senses the un-ceasing struggle of a tortured soul. For a whole year she drifted through the slough of shameful circum-stance, endeavoring in a mad whirl of excitement to harden her nature to her state, in the abandonment of license to find oblivion or distraction. But in vain— in vain! The nights avenged the days; her dead baby came to her in dreams, lay in her bosom as she slept, touched her with its tiny hands, filled her empty arms; the ghost of her slaughtered love rose up stainless beside her darker deeds; even the dumb creatures she had known called to her from afar, and drew anear and looked at her with wistful eyes as if they grieved for her lost condition; through the loudest revelry she heard her child's moaning wail, and could not shut out with wine or wassail from her inward sight the last look of its dying eyes. There was no escaping from the witness within her; she fought the incarnate spirit with every carnal weapon, but the still, small voice could not be silenced; and at last there grew upon her such a horror of her course, such a loathing of herself, such a longing for emancipation from evil doings and disgraceful ties, that she sank into a brooding melancholy that, without speech, irritated and reproached her companions. And then these women, who had rescued her in madness, nursed her in illness, ministered to her in want, buried her baby—scoffed at her sadness, satirized her scruples, jeered and jested at the signs of lingering principle. Gratitude gave her endurance; she could never, never forget that they had once been kind and tender and true. So one day she called them all together, told them in touching words that she must go out from them, must belong to them no more; parted among them all she had gained in that unhappy year of dress and trinkets, embraced them all over and over, and went forth in her old faded robe to seek for work and peace. But work was not to be found; at the old places where they knew and pitied her once, they asked for her record now, and would have none of her; and she discovered too that some change in the times had

made the field scanty and the laborers many; so she
passed through a hard probation of starvation and distress that assailed her with temptation, and tried her
through and through, soul and body. She fancied that
her own self-scorn was reflected in every one's eyes and
echoed in every voice, till she was almost filled with a
dread of human beings, yet in her terrible loneliness
craved something to solace her yearning solitude. And
then she bethought her of the farm-creatures she had
loved; they were not human, and cared not if the
caressing hand belonged to sinner or to saint, and perhaps they had not forgotten her; for though it seemed
so long ago to her, it had really been but a little while
in the calendar of men since she had been with them.
So she had gone all that long distance just to look
again upon the fields where her childhood had been
spent, and to seek a little grain of comfort from the
animals she had fed and nurtured. It was such a little
hope left out of all that life had once had for her! and
it cost her some last sacrifice and left her penniless.
She had been to the familiar meadows, where she had
made hay and picked clover in the past where the
peace of God which passeth understanding rested in
4*

the sunshine and stillness, and soothed her mind and
nerves; but the dogs had barked at her, the lambs fled
away from her, the cows looked at her with unconscious eyes, and a strange farm-hand had driven her off
as an intruding tramp. The dumb creatures had forgotten her; she was so changed by her sin and her sorrow;
she knew all of them, but she had become only a stranger, even to the dun Alderney she had reared up from
birth.

And now she was going back to the great city to find
her baby's grave, and die there—death was the only
merciful thing in this world for such as she!   Only, as
she had passed on her footsore way through this sweet
town, she had suddenly seen the Young Mother and
her Baby sitting at the window; all her heart leaped
up at the sight—it was the first baby she had seen since
her own was taken from her.   Some invisible power
seemed to draw her across the street; she thought if
she could only touch the little hands, press the little
face, it would be like a blessing to her!   That to kiss
once more a baby's pure lips would be like the baptism
of Christ, though her sins were scarlet as blood!   And
now, more than that had come to her—more than had

ever come to her in her life before—a good woman had
put her arms about her, and had not spurned her, because she too had been a mother! But oh! let her go
now—let her go—it was more than she could bear—let
her go to her own baby!

The Young Mother had listened with tears running
down her cheeks; in her heart of hearts she had felt
that every word was truth, and never before in her
love-sheltered existence had she realized the wickedness
and wretchedness of a world outside her own. As she
listened, she had thought—thought with reason contend-
ing with that charity which overcometh all things—
should she keep her, this waif from the under-world of
vice, this woman torn with suffering, strife, and repentance? Should she hold her fast as a precious soul to
be saved from wrath to come? or should she send her
forth again from a haven of refuge and safety to fresh
hardship, contumely, and suicide, and so have before
her conscience an accusing figure forever and forever?
Could she bring her young sisters into the atmosphere
of one so tainted? Could she trust her child with one
who had been dragged through the mud of the earth?

Was sin contagious from the body? Ah! her little
babe had lain in those stained arms, had smiled in that
face, and had taken no harm. Was it infectious from
the spirit? Surely this woman's soul was purified by
penitence! Only speech and action could convey evil;
could she not guard against that? Ought she not to
give her a trial? Would it not be time enough to turn
her away when her influence proved corrupt? Should
she help her? Should she save her? Dared she, who
was happy, and had her own Baby safe, thrust out
another, who was most miserable, and whose baby was
dead? Whose baby was dead! Her tears welled out—
the charity that overcometh had won the day. She was
no longer to her a sinner, an outcast, a Magdalen, but
only a mother whose baby was dead.

And when the other said more quietly, "You know
all now; you can only think badly of me like all the
rest!" she took the thin hands in hers, and answered,
"I think you have been more sinned against than
sinning, and that the dear Father in Heaven has
brought you to me. Will you stay with me, and take
care of my Baby? I have great need of some
one who will put love into this work, and maybe

after a while my little one will comfort you for your
own."

Surprised by this unexpected offer, she, to whom
kindness was so unusual, looked up as one astounded.
" You will take me?" she said slowly ; "you will keep
me? You will give me your Baby?"

" I will give you more," replied the Young Mother.
"I will give you Love and a Great Trust. And you
can help or harm me much ; for if you are loyal and
faithful to me and yourself, you will give me a larger
and surer confidence in all humanity ; but if you do
not deal righteously and truly with me, I shall never
dare to listen to the voice of my own soul again! You
see it is an experiment for both."

The woman bowed down her head, and there was
silence between them for a minute. Then she lifted
her eyes with a new light in them : " I could not have
dreamed there was anything left for me in this world
to do!" she answered. " I will live, since you do not
think me unworthy of such a trust, if only to try and
prove to you that there is something true in me still!
I will stay with you. I will be faithful."

And as a sign and token of their compact, the Young

Mother lifted Baby from its crib, and laid her on the other's breast. "Oh, *my* baby! my own baby!" she broke out, "I *must* see my baby's grave!"

"Not now, dear," said the Young Mother. "I cannot let you leave me yet. Some day we will go there together!"

The whole family, as they came in and out, passed judgment on the New Nurse. When the Young Father found her installed in his home, he privately remarked to his wife that she looked rather delicate for such a weight as Baby was getting to be; and the Young Mother put her arms about him, and replied: "Dearest love, she has had hard times; we will make her stronger among us; and just see how Baby takes to her!" and she never told him any more than that, she who kept nothing else hid from him all through her life. Grandfather Number Two said he "was glad that Baby had got any kind of a nurse at last, so that he could hear something else talked about!" But Grandfather Number One studied the pale face more than once as he played with Baby; and one day, when the Young Mother went with him out of the room, he put

his arms round her and bade "God bless her for a good
lass! For there has been a sore life in there," he said,
"and she is finding peace with my dear girl!" "Oh,
papa!" she whispered, "how do you know?" "I know
nothing of your Nurse," he answered, "but I can tell
a good work when I see it!" "Oh, papa, papa!" she
murmured; "it isn't me; it is all the Baby! don't you
see that it is Baby who is healing and helping her?"
and Grandfather Number One laid her face against his
for a moment, and went quietly forth. The Grandmothers were inclined to be decidedly critical at first,
in consequence of ineffectual visits to the Intelligence
Offices, and from disapproval of taking in a servant
without a reference; but they could not help but notice
her patience and loving care of her charge, and when
they beheld her sewing were completely won over, and
went about proclaiming her a treasure. And the
Young Aunties wondered that she shrank from them a
little, and was so shy when they were so gay and gracious with her; but Baby loved her—that was evident
enough—and so they were determined to be good to
her; and soon after the faded dress had been taken
away by the Young Mother, and destroyed entirely

from being a reminder of the past, Baby's Nurse was many times overcome with thoughtful little gifts of collars and cuffs, aprons and ribbons, and generous overflowings of young and gushing hearts. While from the Poor Relation, whose instinctive sympathy divined that here was one who sorrowed greatly, there came sometimes such gentle words of strength, such uphold-ing of the sinking spirit, that the tried soul clung to her saving grace as though this other woman had indeed been a holy priest ordained of God. And the Fat Nurse, dropping in one day with her basket and um-brella, watched her keenly with her twinkling eyes, and said afterwards to the Young Mother, "You've did well by your Baby, mum; for she's got the Mother-heart, and that's the best recommendation any nurse can have!"

One day, when the following Spring had made all the earth green, the Young Mother and the New Nurse went away to the great city, passing through its noise and bustle to another city on its quiet borders, whose people were very still in their last homes—the silent City of the Dead; and among the lowly graves of the poor found a little mound grown over with waving grass and golden buttercups; and what befell there of remembrance and remorse, of weeping and consolation, gratitude and goodness, the two women locked up in their hearts, and never spoke of again; but, before they came away, the lonely grave was covered over with myrtle, and set round with roses, and when next they saw it there was a small white stone at the head, on which was only cut, " In memory of a Baby," for this child had died without a name.

And the New Nurse lived all her long years with them, and kept her promise, and was faithful to the end. ꞌ She came to be like one of their own family, and was respected and trusted, loved and looked up to. It was she who took all their new-born childen in her arms, and tenderly laid out all their dead; she dressed the young for their bridals, and closed the eyes of the old; she rejoiced in their joy, sorrowed with their sorrow, shared their burdens; and the next generation never thought but that she had always been one of them. A weird sort of wisdom from much introspection fell on her, and many an earnest word of hers took root for salvation in restless or wayward hearts; fruits meet for repentance marked all her unassuming way; her eyes shone with a beautiful peace; and she who had been cast down and desolate, made gladness for the angels in heaven.

Many years afterwards, when Baby had grown to be a young lady, when the Young Father had become a rich and renowned citizen and the Young Mother a wise and well-beloved matron, much courted in the social life of the great city where she visited, she met the man who had wrought this ruin, prosperous and debonair, esteemed and honored, the cynosure of fashion, head and front of his admiring circle still. It struck him with strange novelty and curious wonder that this one woman, so sought after and distinguished, should meet him always with cold eyes, or turn from him with averted glances. It made him uneasy, this Epicurean who shrank from a crumpled rose-leaf, and that any one human being should disdain or discountenance him was a skeleton at his life-long feast that must speedily be banished. So, watching one night at a great assembly till he had seen her a little apart, with the graceful effrontery of a practised man of the world, he ventured to question her of the why and thus. She turned her sweet, fair face full upon him all kindling with long-kept indignation and contempt, and spoke out from her sincere heart the stinging answer: "For twenty years I have sheltered in my house the woman whose life you ruined, whose youth you destroyed; and I therefore deem you unworthy even of her scorn! Seducer and profligate! You are loathsome as a lie! and I forbid you ever to approach or speak to me again!" He winced and writhed under her righteous anger and plain-spoken words, that like a sharp knife had cut into his vanity and his memory; he slipped away from her speechless and cowed; and whether or not his conscience ever reproached him with remorseful remembrances, he never forgot the crumpled roseleaf in his career—the expressed odium of one honest spirit.

And never in all the days of her life did this true woman breathe to any one else, Father or Mother, husband, sister or child, that other woman's secret of a Baby's Grave.

V.

On her bed she lay day after day, year in and year out, white and helpless, with large eyes melancholy with the sadness of long suffering. Only the unwearied hands rested not, and the active brain never ceased from thinking. What dreams of health and happiness, what disappointed hopes, what unspoken repinings, what agonies of despair, what rebellious reflections, what wrestlings with destiny, what strivings for patience, had been worked off upon the exquisite embroidery that grew under her delicate fingers! for always before her was a snowy, diaphanous muslin, with its fine tracery of leaves and flowers, vines and fruit, and into every branch and every blossom she wove her life, and by the perfectly wrought designs she won the cost of her living. One day it would be a lovely wedding-dress that was spread over her humble couch, and out of her tender blessings on the bride, her sweet fancies of a bliss she could never know, there would be evolved a wonderful result of interwoven beauty, with a poetic meaning in it all that perhaps the wearer would never guess ; and only the worker, touching gently her undivined creation, would know that each design was significant of a good wish—the lilies for purity, the roses for love, the wheat for plenty, the heart's-ease for content. Or it would be an infant's robe to be made rich and rare with unrivalled adornment, and little would the pleased mother suspect the yearnings over the untried future and the visions of its coming life that were wrought through and through her child's dainty garment ; how upon each thread-born wreath there hung prayers for the coming years, and how every festoon had felt the prophetic outlook of a solitary spirit to whom a new-born babe seemed like an angel fresh from God, to be once more, when earthly career was over, a bearer of palm-branches in the universal heaven. Or, once in a while, they would bring her a spotless shroud to fashion for the dead, and would find unexpectedly laid upon it some mystic emblem to grace the grave, an amaranth or a winged globe, to symbolize to hearts that looked thereon the sweet everlasting Beyond. For never unto others went forth the bitterness of tortured flesh or prisoned existence; the white roses that she raised were the flowers of silence; the womanhood that was in her naturally taught her repression; the unselfishness of her spirit held her back from saddening others; and her Thought of God and want of outer experience gave her a trust and faith that could overcome at last her weariness, her isolation, her doubts. But there were times— oh! there were times when the frail body went through the very Valley of the Shadow of Death; when the pain, the impotence, the unquiet of a separated lot would stir the tried soul with inward storms of revolt and longing; when the unuttered heart-cries were as piercing and tempestuous in unseen ears as those of a strong man in his agony. But Love was about her always; and, as unto those to whom little is given, spontaneous gratitude is great for that little—the suffusing glow of thankfulness for returning ease, the throb of sincere joy at a new attention, the bursting of sunlight into her room, the sight of the calm, blue sky, the sound of a tender voice, would still the tumult, and through the shining point of her needle her discontent would

flow into lines of beauty, and peace would return with
the needed pursuit, and by counting over her pleasures
she conquered her pain. For much and many ministered to her. The Aged Father and Mother added to
her wisdom, poured out for her the hoary experiences
of accumulated years, caressed her with their withered
hands, shone upon her with their wrinkled faces, where
affection beamed brighter than their eyes; and she, who
was the Poor Relation in other homes, but the Light of
the Household here, she never tired in her tendence;
she who, without a word, knew all that passed within
the kindred mind, whose sweet sympathy soothed, whose
genial cheerfulness uplifted, whose arms were around
her in the night-watches of suffering, whose days never
brought forgetfulness of a single loving care, and who
was at once Sister, Friend, and Physician of soul and
body. Then there were those abroad who came to her
in kindness, often bringing gifts of thoughtfulness and
overflowing compassion. The Grandfathers would
come, thumping their gold-headed canes upon the floor
and her nerves, with hearty salutations, and the very
breath of fresh outer air on their portly persons and
ruddy faces; and the chirpy Grandmothers, with their

gossipy talk of the younger generation, and something
nice to tempt the delicate taste, made from an old family receipt that none possessed but themselves. And
the Young Aunties, by twos and threes—bright and beautiful with youth, full of lightness and mirth, gleeful
with girlhood's quips and quirks, and always ready to
relate all that was going on in their happy world—the
last party, the latest fashion, the newest books, blushing
confidences, tremulous hopes, sometimes the sentimental
woes and imaginary ills; sure always of a cordial lis-
tener and faithful adviser, and rarely thinking that their
gayety and grace might cause a pang to one to whom
youth and beauty and the world beyond her chamber-
walls were evermore denied. Then her bird sang for
her such a delicious song that it awakened marvellous
harmonies within, and was sometimes echoed by strains
unheard of mortal ears; for that one voice concentrated
for her the chorussed music of the groves; the liquid
notes linked themselves to the harmony of the spheres,
and an awe-inspiring refrain of cherubim and seraphim
seemed to float to her from the far-off Everlasting!
And when the little golden songster tucked his head
under his wing at night, her fancy went out all over the

earth, and saw in all climes birds of all kinds and plu-
mage nestling into slumber, and her eyes filled with
yearning tears over these feathered innocents, which
were thus her only link with God's dumb creatures.
And as she gazed out of her window at the small patch
of sky she could see therefrom, the floating clouds wore .
varied shapes for her—shapes beautiful or fantastic, making always a changing panorama of which she never tired.
Sometimes it was a dark dragon, with overlapping scales
and forked tongue ; anon a soft, gray vision of clustered
towers and spires ; and again weird and witching faces
would form and dissolve against the serene blue ; sometimes a white angel with outspread wings would hover
over her, and sometimes the sunset glories would make
a gorgeous garden of heavenly blossoms before her eyes ;
but oftenest a snowy dove would brood in the great im-
mensity, and then she felt as if the Spirit filled her
heart and mind, and lifted her in aspiration till she was
no longer a crippled and pain-stricken body, but only a
chosen soul taken behind the veil of flesh and sense to
behold the secret mysteries of being. Thus in her quiet
room, in the silence and solitude of a separated life, she
was neither desolate, nor despairing, nor deprived of the
5

solace which the good God gives to all who have hearts to feel. But, nevertheless, one thing troubled her much: others did so much for her; some one, it seemed to her, was always bringing her help or pleasure; but there was so little she could do for any one! Her Father in Heaven was loving and bountiful in His mercies to her, but there was nothing she could do for Him! Praise Him, like her bird, she sometimes did from the very depths of her nature; but she longed, almost infinitely at times, to reach out towards His children on the earth, and repay to them her debt to Him. In her own home the proceeds of her daily work assisted in maintaining the life that was there, and secured her from becoming a burden upon much-taxed and slender resources. But still this was so little, so little, and she knew not how to do more, her world was so narrow and she came in contact with so few. Her heart was full as a fountain of its waters, but she had no direction in which to pour out the overflow; the sacred hour of opportunity had not arrived—the right chord had not yet been struck.

One day they sent the Baby to see her—the bright-eyed, rosy-mouthed Baby, with the little golden rings of

hair fringing the dainty cap, and the tiny dimpled hand
stretching out to her from beneath the embroidered cape
of the long cloak. It was almost the only Baby she
remembered ever to have known, for the young Aunties were not born in her neighborhood, and it was so
long since there had been a baby in the family. Instantly a new tenderness and vague yearning sprang up
in her soul; perhaps the woman's regret that never,
never would the blessing of Motherhood be hers, mingled with the other expressions on her pale face;
perhaps too there was something more which told that
only alone, could the lonely spirit grapple with and
overcome these unusual emotions, for Baby's Nurse,
wise from her own experiences, quietly took off Baby's
wraps, laid the soft white-robed creature in her arms,
and went swiftly from the room. She remained away
but a little while, not long enough to tire too much the
fragile arms; but in that time the Crippled Sister had
shed drops and drops of shining tears over the placid
Baby, who looked up at her with strangely wise eyes, not
frightened at her unfamiliar face, but as if also pondering the secret things of the heart, for babies sometimes
seem so freshly come from Paradise, that either mem-

ories or meditation over unseen marvels appear to hold
them in temporary stillness and contemplation, and
to give a sense of speechless knowledge past our understanding who have come so far away from the wonder-
world which is the source of life and light.

"O Baby, Baby!" she said, in her very heart of hearts,
"you are a miracle! for you are a soul—one of God's
souls born into this world—this world where souls struggle and suffer! How I wish—oh, how I wish that I,
even I, crippled and useless, could stand between you
and all the pain of the future! Sweet, tender blossom,
dear innocent birdie, why cannot you always be a
Baby? why must you grow up to be crowned with
thorns, to be crucified, as every soul must be, before you
go back to that other life! Blessings may come to you—
blessings will come to you, for you are the Baby of love
and hope; but oh, you new-made darling! you have
come into a hard world, for you have been born a
woman!"

For it suddenly seemed to the Crippled Sister as if
she had never before so keenly felt or fancied the strife,
the poverty, the crime of this earth, as when she looked
upon this untried, sinless being, and there dawned upon

her a sudden terrible dream of the might be of any
human existence; all the agony and rebellion of her
own years rolled up, and momentarily smote down her
long patience, but out of it arose a longing almost divine, to shelter, to shield, not this one only, but all
young and untainted lives from the wrath and evil to
come. With that singular outlook born of solitude and
imagination, she beheld countless homes where babies
bloomed—babies, all to be men and women some day—
and she shuddered as she thought what men and women
were in the world, and how even the sweetest and
purest knew sorrow and needed strength. And she—
she who would fain have suffered, in her great hour of
yearning over a baby and her race, that the many might
be made white from their sins again—what could she
do? What could she do? It seemed to her as if she
was the smallest, most useless, most impotent creation
in the Universe, lying there growing almost weary'
under the weight of a single mortal Baby. But the
child was God's angel and brought His message! She
always said afterwards, if it had not been for the Baby
she never would have gained the idea, for as Baby lay
quite still looking solemnly up at her, thoughts and

plans flashed in upon her like electric sparks struck from the innocent presence.

In a few minutes it had all come into her mind, clear and vivid as a reading of God's word; the Baby's little hand had touched the waiting chord; through the Baby's pure eyes she had seen her opportunity; the Baby had given her at last a work to do for her Father in Heaven and her race on earth. And as if this Baby had divined that its mission was ended, and as if it had just dawned upon its infantile sense that the glowing face bending over its own was that of neither Mother nor Nurse, it set up a very human cry, and the latter came in, put on the long white cloak, held up the pouting mouth to be kissed by pale, quivering lips, and carried her charge away, pondering in her own heart what manner of emotions the Child had awakened in the Crippled Sister's spirit.

A few days afterwards the Light of the Household went forth into the poor places of the neighborhood, and brought in, one by one, shrinking children, with shabby garments and shy glances; little girls ungathered into schools, untaught of ignorant parents who were slaves of labor, to whom was preached no Gospel of salvation from idleness, weakness, or vice. These, allured in unwillingly at first, hard enough for a time to keep together, came at last into this quiet chamber as to a holy shrine, sat earnestly at the feet of a pale, patient teacher, and learned the ways of truth and right, took from her untiring zeal a shield of work or wisdom to defend them in days to come from dependence, debasement, and ruin. Day by day—for a few minutes only sometimes, sometimes for hours, according to her fluctuating strength—she had them with her, pouring out the garnered stores of unforgotten reading in simple language, and opening up new worlds for unformed minds; peopling for them with her sweet fancy the woods, the streams, the air, with as beautiful spiritings as the old fantastic shapes of pagan lore; showing them what she saw in the sky; telling them what her bird sang to her, breathing into their receptive souls the peace and good-will that angels hymn to mankind, clothing common facts in such attractive forms that knowledge grew to be better than choice gold, and making labor so sacred and honorable in their eyes, that to do seemed well as to be wise. It was slow work, slow and anxious and earnest, taking more

patience than the bearing of pain, calling upon the
deepest founts of love for all the charity that suffereth
long and hopeth all things; for ignorance, habit, and
inherited traits are formidable fortresses to assail, and
can only be overcome by continuance in well-doing.
Clumsy fingers and unopened minds were equally diffi-
cult to guide and to train; but when the heart was
once won the will grew strong, and out of her untiring
effort came evidence of fine fruition at last.

In the poor homes where they belonged the mothers
listened with a sort of awe to the accounts of this pale
lady, lying always on her couch, covered with the white,
fleecy folds of her delicate work, and giving out to
little rapt listeners thoughts that would abide with them
all their lives; and the first result of this feeling was
clean faces and smooth pinafores. Then the children's
talk brought new ideas to the laboring fathers that
brightened the weary toil, and something gentler
seemed to steal into the hard and bare existences, and
so the sweet influences radiated farther than she could
feel, and her work was wider than she knew.

After a while Christmas was drawing near, and one
day there was an interesting assemblage of these small

scholars in a room where one of them lived, whose
mother was a washerwoman, and upon tubs and
buckets they were seated in a circle, with their childish
countenances expressive of anxious meditation. The
weather was cold, and the devices to secure warmth,
mostly consisting of capes and shawls belonging to
grown-up people and much too large for their present
wearers, gave them generally the appearance of ani-
mated bundles with a face at one end, and the tips of
very worn shoes—sometimes of bare toes, peeping out
of the other; and the subject of their meeting and consultation was, How to Get a Christmas Present for the
Crippled Sister, and What It Should Be.

No thought of expediency or custom entered these
youthful and inexperienced minds; it was a matter of
pure love and gratitude, or as one of them put it,
"She's bin mighty good and lovin' to us, and we want to
do suthin' to make her feel we know it!" The leader
of the meeting was a grave little damsel with quiet eyes,
who seemed to take a natural precedence. "Now,
Anner Mariar," she said to a buzzing wee thing beside
her, "there ain't no use in guessin' and talkin' so
much; let's count up; each girl say how much she can
5*

give; we've got to know that first of all. You begin, Anner Mariar; how much are you goin' to have by Christmas?"

"Well," chirped out this small being from the folds of a large red muffler, "I'm a goin' to settle down and take a place to mind Mrs. M'Goffin's baby next door; it's an awful big baby, and drefful cross, but I guess I kin do it, and get my share for the teacher! I'm to have twenty-five cents a week, but I have to give Mam most of it, cos' I can't work out, and go to the Lady's, and help her too! but I kin save five cents a week off anyhow! It ain't much, but it's better'n nothin', and Lord knows I'll earn it with that baby!"

"There now, Anner Mariar, that'll do; let somebody else say something, will you?" interposed the youthful President. "Jane O'Connor, what do you think you'll have?"

The O'Connor's child wound herself very tight in a big plaid shawl. "I'm goin' to do chores in the mornin' for a boardin'-house, carry up the coals and sich, and they're to pay me ten cents a day. I spec' the old man will take a good deal of it for gin, but I mean to screw a quarter of it out anyhow, if I have to fight for it!"

"So far so good," observed the approving Chief.
"Nettie Blane, it's your turn!" Nettie looked down
abashed by the superior facilities of her companions,
and spoke in a rather low and tremulous tone. "I
ain't likely to have a chance to earn any money; but
Uncle Jim—he's a sailor, you know—he brought me two
lovely shells home from his last voyage; they're all
smooth and pink inside, such a beautiful color, and
have got scolloped edges just like lace, and I thought
maybe I could sell them!" Hereupon ensued an ani-
mated discussion as to the probability of the market
value of these treasures, and much advice as to places
where there would be most likelihood of disposing of
them. Little Nettie's checks flushed as pink as the
shells themselves with excitement over the subject, and
her youthful soul experienced the first pain and joy of
sacrifice.

Then the question of resources was put to each of
the others in turn, and each made some hopeful reply.
One had an uncle who always gave her something for
Christmas, and she thought she could coax him to present it a few days beforehand ; and one had a tin bank
into which she had dropped all the few pennies she had

received for two or three years, and she was willing to contribute all of them; and so on through the whole group, till a rough estimate was made by the grave little President, after much struggling with the arithmetical problem, and the financial committee rose up from the tubs and buckets in quite tumultuous delight at the amount of the uncollected sum. They circled round for some minutes in rather noisy glee, till the small Chief called them unceremoniously to order by standing on a tub and exclaiming:

"Look here! We have found out How To Do It, but we haven't made up our minds yet What It Is To Be!" There was an immediate subsidence at this suggestion, and the important deliberation was resumed. This was a very serious question indeed, as it was no longer a matter requiring individual responsibility, but a general decision and consent, and the tone of the discussion became much more argumentative. "What It Should Be" was one of those puzzles requiring experience in intuition to decide, and wild and extravagant were some of the first propositions by the more thoughtless and those uninitiated into the cost of things. "I tell you what," said Anna Maria, "there's nothin' like a big cake! there was one stayed in the baker's window ever so long till last Christmas, and it was all over shinin' white icin', and it had a yaller and a red and a blue rose right on top; and oh, my! it was just splendid. I used to stand and stand and stand and look at it till my toes were a-most froze, just a-thinkin' what an awful lot of nice eatin' there was in it! Now, *I* say let *It* be a cake, for it's so good and so Christmassy!'"

"Anner Marier," remarked the small President, "you're just crazy! Have you any idear what that cake cost? Besides, the Lady gets enough to eat, and *she* isn't the sort as is always thinking of her stomach."

Anna Maria was quenched for a moment, but retained a sense of injury at being thus unceremoniously snubbed, which only waited for an opportunity to be vented.

Directly the O'Connor's child observed that *she* thought it would be nice to give the Lady a whole lot of fine thread for her work, because she used so much all the time.

"Thread!" contemptuously retorted Anna Maria, "who ever heard tell of thread for a Christmas present!"

"It's a heap more useful ñor a cake!" replied the other.

"Pooh!" said Anna Maria, "people never gets useful things at Christmas, only something pretty to look at, and good things to eat."

"Well, anyhow, I guess she wouldn't care about a cake!"

"I bet she would'then!"

"She wouldn't!"

"She would!"

"Hold yer tongue!" "I won't!" "Then take that!" and the O'Connor's child gave Anna Maria a quick slap on the cheek. Anna Maria, not having been trained in the Scripture doctrine of turning the other cheek when she was smitten once, was about to return the blow, when the little Chief, with her face all aglow, stepped in between the excited parties.

"Ain't you ashamed of yourselves, after all the blessed things the Lady's bin teaching us! Didn't she read us out of the Good Book one day, 'Little children, love one another!' and talk to us about it till we couldn't most of us a-help crying? And you two ain't no better nor you had never heard it at all! Do you think she'd

care about a cake, or anything at all, if she knew you'd
bin fighting over it? Now, you just kiss and make up,
and don't have no more such sass!" And Anna Maria
and the O'Connor's child were quite overcome, and fell
upon each other's necks and kissed, and then sat lovingly
down together on the same tub.

Then, after this, strange and various articles were
proposed, to which many objections were raised, princi-
pally by the little President, who seemed to think her
most important duty was to keep the intended expendi-
ture within the limits of the probable amount, for
which purpose she was obliged to do a good many sums
out loud. The puzzle was growing deeper, and the
likelihood of a decision seemed farther off than ever,
when Nettie Blane said, in her soft voice: "I know
what the Lady loves more than anything else, and that's
flowers! Why, just here awhile ago, before it got so
cold, I found a bunch of wild posies growing alongside
the road as I was going to her house; they were just
common things, but I picked them and took them to
her, and you just ought to have seen her over them!
Her face lit all up, she was so pleased, and do you know
that for a minute she looked like she never was sick at

all; and she kind of petted them with her fingers, and
thanked me so nice that I never was so glad of doing
anything in my life! Now, don't you all think she'd
rather have flowers—real nice flowers, I mean, like you
see young gentlemen taking to their sweethearts; not
anything we could find, but something we'd have to
buy?"

The unconscious poetry in this little girl's soul had
vaguely divined that material gifts were not delicate
enough for this lonely spirit who communed with things
unseen. Nettie's earnestness enforced her idea, which
seemed to impress the fancies of her companions, till
one exclaimed:

"But flowers die so soon, and then she would never
have nothin' to keep to make her feel that we'd bin
thinkin' of her!"

An anxious shade fell over Nettie Blane's face, that
however instantly brightened with a new thought.

"Oh, yes she would," she said, "because she'd
always remember! Don't you know, somehow, if you
once get a thing, you've always got it, even if you don't
see it! If I sell my shells, it don't much matter really,
because whenever I think about them they'll always be

in my heart, and I'll always know that Uncle Jim he brought them to me over the sea!"

The wise intuitions of the little philosopher struck the poetic chord in the small surrounding humans. Some one murmured, "Things ought to be awful pretty to be remembered always!" and the general consent seemed to settle without dispute that a basket of flowers would be the very sweetest thing in the world to give.

"And I know of a man who keeps a hot-house just out of town," said the young President, "and he looks good-humored and kind, so maybe he'll give us something real nice for what we'll have to pay!" And soon after the meeting dispersed, each one going her way, with the sense of quite an important aim embellishing the future.

The day before Christmas, as the big, burly and rosy owner of the conservatory just out of town was sorting his choicest blooms for a large wedding which was to take place in the evening, with a deftness hardly to have been expected from the size of his fingers, the door of the hot-house suddenly opened, and a squadron of a dozen or more small girls, headed by a grave-eyed little damsel, entered in solemn procession.

"Bless my soul!" said the Gentle Giant, turning his bluff, bright face towards them," what do you young ones want ?"

For an instant ·they had stood quite still, looking about them in wonder and delight; for the whole place was so filled with rare, and lovely blossoms that its atmosphere, color, and profusion was like a concentration of the tropics. Anna Maria nudged the O'Connor's child to look at yellow oranges ripening amid their own foliage, and murmured, "Oh, my! they're really growin' there, they are!" And Nettie Blanc's tender gaze lingered on the white camellias and clustered azaleas, as if for the first time in her life she had realized a fulfilled sense of perfect beauty. But the Young Leader, deeply impressed with the importance of her errand, had never taken her eyes off the hearty countenance of the Big Gardener, and was not to be diverted from its practical pursuit by any allurements of tint or odor, and in her quiet voice replied to his surprised salutation :

"If you please, sir, we want to buy a basket of flowers."

The man dropped the two or three buds he held in his hand, turned entirely around, and gave one steady look down the whole line; he saw at once that they were not likely to want flowers for themselves, and imagined that one or two had been sent on a message, and that the rest had accompanied these.

" *You*—want—to—*buy* "—he said slowly.

" Yes, sir, a basket of flowers, if you please.

" Who for? and why are there so many of you ? "

" Well, sir, I'll tell you. · You see, sir, there's a dear, kind Lady, and she's a cripple, and never gets off a low kind of bed she lays on, and works all the time the most beautiful broidering flowers you ever seen. And she teaches us; we go there to her room, and she tells us—oh! she tells us such sweet things about everything, and she tries to make us good, and we're learning ever so much from her. So we thought we'd like to give her a Christmas present, and we've all saved up till we think we've got enough; and because she never can go out to see anything a-growing, and just loves flowers like they were alive, we made up our minds to take her some; because we all give something towards it we all came together about it; and if you please, sir,

we'd.like as nice a basketful as you can make up for
our money."

The rosy face bloomed out bright as one of his own
blossoms; the round eyes grew wonderfully soft and
moist, as the big, burly man stooped and kissed the
small speaker, and said, with just a touch of huskiness
in his voice:

"Well, you're a blessed little party! You just go
round, all of you, and pick out what you'd like to have,
and I'll fix them up for you!" There was an immediate stir in the young procession, an evident delight in
this permission, and an intention to put it instantly
into practice, when the Small Leader called out, "You
keep still there, will you? Iv'e got something else to
say!"

Curiosity restored order, and she again addressed the
gardener.

"Ain't those grand flowers very dear? You see, sir,
we don't want anything we can't pay for all right;
because, you know, if you were to go and put in out of
goodness something that ought to cost more than we've
got the money for, it would be you a-giving, not us!
Besides, if it was too fine, the Lady would be worried

with thinking where we'd got enough to do it with ! So
if you will please to give us something as nice as you
can for just what we can pay for it, we will be so much
obliged. We've got this much money ; please to count
it, sir, and see if it will do ! " And she handed him a
rather battered tin match-box containing the accumulated contributions in small coins, as they had been
gradually brought in as they were gained.

And as the Gentle Giant took the minute box in his
big hands he had to cough to keep down an uncomfort-
able choking in his throat, and which became even
more troublesome when Nettie Blane stepped up to
him, and said : " If we can afford it, sir, could you put
in a Lily ? because it seems as if she ought to have
white flowers, and I know she loves lilies because she
always sets so many of them in her work ; and I heard
her say one day—like to herself—that Solomon in all
his glory was not arrayed like one of these ! "

The Big Gardener by this time was too much touched
to keep quite calm. " Here," he said to the Little
Leader, " you count out this money, and tell me how
much it is, and I'll do the best I can for it ! " As the
grave voice enumerated the amount, piece by piece,

the rest looked and listened with an eager pride in the limited sum which was pathetic to behold, as every penny of it had been earned by some sort of sacrifice. And when the Big Gardener took a basket and went round his hot-house collecting here and there his simplest blooms, all these keen eyes watched him in unbroken silence, and not one of them stirred a gaze from his fingers as he laid in the moss, propped a superb, stainless lily in the centre, and arranged round it with exquisite taste, violets and heart's-ease, and delicate, pure blossoms; in breathless quiet they noted every flower that was woven into its place, little thinking that these commoner plants which they were used to see in summer were almost as costly as foreign growths in winter; and it was not till the whole was finished that they broke out into exclamations of satisfaction.

"This must be a mighty good woman to make you love her so!" said the man as he handed over the basket to the careful hold of the Little Leader.

"Good!" answered Nettie Blane, "she's a-most an angel; it seems like she ought never to do anything but stand up close to the Throne with just such lilies in her hand!"

For Nettie's inmost heart was stirred by the flowers and the occasion.

The Big Gardener looked at her a second as if he thought she might have been a stray cherub herself.

" That's all your own gift," he said,·pointing to the lily-crowned basket; " but would you mind taking her a little present from me too ? "

There was a pause in general fear lest his superior resources might eclipse the glory of their own offering; the Gentle Giant smiled and answered the unexpressed thought.

" It shall only be one flower," he said; and as a single flower in their inexperienced eyes could not possibly compare with a basketful, a happy assent was immediately given.

He went round among his plants to where bloomed one magnificent blossom, the only one of its kind in the greenhouse. For months and months he had nurtured this particular growth with the utmost care, training it towards the production of this one flower ·with the solicitude of a father for a child, knowing that its rarity and splendor would bring an immense price; but now, with a glowing face, he broke it unhesitatingly from the stalk, and without a sensation of regret, placed it in Nettie Blanc's hand. "Oh, thank you!" said Nettie's glad voice, "I will give it to her with your compliments." And then the Big Gardener kissed every one of them as they passed out, and stood at his hot-house door, and watched the little procession as it wound out of sight with the Little Leader at the head, carrying the Basket of Flowers.

The Crippled Sister was lying on her low couch, working a butterfly on a white shroud—for the dead know not Christmas, and wait for no one's holiday; and as the emblem of immortality spread its wings beneath her glancing needle, she crooned over to herself the song that the angels sang to the wondering shepherds so many centuries ago; and as the "Good will towards men" dropped from her lips, her chamber door opened and the Light of The Household entered in, followed by the procession of children bearing their precious burden. The Light of The Household had tears in her eyes and a quiver about her mouth as she said, "Dear Sister, the little ones have brought you a Christmas present!" for she had met them at the hall-door, and divined all the sweet story from their few words of explanation.

Then the Little Leader stepped forward with the basket of flowers, and as the Crippled Sister took it in her hands the shroud fell aside, but even in the living delight of the Present, the butterfly of Immortality rested on her bosom below the shining flower of the Annunciation; and as the children stood round the bed in their poor clothes, and some of their hands hardened by toil, it dawned upon her how they had worked and sacrificed to bring her this token of love, and her heart was almost too full for words, and tears of purest, saddest joy dropped like rain upon the violets and heart's-ease that represented to her the tender gratitude of those innocent souls. " It is so beautiful ! so beautiful ? " she murmured, and they fairly thrilled to think she meant their happy gift; but Nettie Blane alone felt that it was of their feelings she spoke, and as if to crown the season's offering of good-will, she laid the single gorgeous blossom beside their own present, saying :

" The Big Garderner sent you this too, ma'am, with his compliments, because he said you ' must be a mighty

6

good woman to make us love you so much.'" Then
the rich color flooded the Crippled Sister's cheek and
brow, and her eyes shone, and she seemed to grow
transfigured before their very sight into angelic youth
and beauty, and her voice was almost like a song as she
cried out, "O my darlings! you have made me so rich
to-day, for you have brought me not only these lovely,
lovely flowers, but something I thought never could
come into my lonely life—the free, blessed Love of
Children!" And she kissed them all over and over,
and when they lingered as though loth to leave her, her
spirit seemed inspired to speak to them from the text
of the flowers; through the Big Gardener's rare blossom she seemed to bring before them the wonders, the
glories, the very atmosphere of the East; they saw the
palms of India and the gardens of Damascus, the roses
of Persia, and the Cedars of Lebanon; and out of the
simple blooms of their own sweet gift, she wove tender
stories and lessons that would cling in their memories
to heart's-ease and violets as long as they lived; and she
told them at last that the great old artists, when they
painted their pictures of the Angel bringing Good News
to Mary, the Mother of Christ, always placed just such

another white Lily in his hand; and that it was sign
and token of message and promise. And somehow, as
she talked, these poor, little, narrow lives felt themselves grow nearer to the angels; and when, after they
had all joined together in singing for her the Christmas
hymn, they went out to their humble homes with their
hearts upraised in "Glory to God on high," because
they felt, in their vague way, that in that one room at
least there was "peace on earth and good-will towards
men."

And the Light of the Household leaned over the
Crippled Sister with a half sob in her tone as she said,
"This is a happy Christmas, Dear!" "Ah! yes," answered she. "And it all came from the precious Baby;
for if it had not been for the Baby, I should never have
thought of these other children! Kneel down, sister,
and say a Christmas prayer for the dear Children and
the darling Baby!"

VI.

BABY'S PARTY.

BABY was going into short frocks; and the Young Aunties had all assembled in Baby's home in order to assist the Young Mother in cutting down the long robes which had hitherto covered Baby's restless little feet. They were a gay and happy party as they sat around the pile of dainty white garments, one ripping, another cutting, and the rest sewing with nimble and willing fingers, while Baby lay in the midst, and greatly interrupted the work and merry chat; for first one Young Auntie would stop to coo back to the chirping crows, and then a general flow of baby talk would suspend the flashing thimbles; then another Young Auntie, having to do a little necessary measuring of Baby's tiny person, must needs dandle the small creature a while to each of the other Aunties, until the fun grew fast and furious, and Baby wild with infantile delight; and then

another Aunty was moved to kiss the rosy mouth because "the little darling was too sweet to live," and all
the other Young Aunties felt called upon to follow suit,
until at last the Young Mother called the party to
order, using her gold thimble as a gavel, and crying out
in a loud voice that she had something important to
say. Curiosity conquered the spirit of frolic, and the
small fetish was left in peace by its feminine worship-
pers until all the say was said; the neglected cambric
was resumed and the bright needles began to fly again
in this charming sewing-circle.

"I have been thinking," spoke the Young Mother,
when some stillness was restored, "that I should like to
celebrate in some way or other Baby's change into short
clothes; suppose we have a Baby party!"

Then the sluices of talk opened up; exclamations
of "Capital!" "Glorious!" "What a nice idea!"
echoed from the Young Aunties, and then began to
flow a stream of plans and suggestions.

"How many babies do we know?" "Shall all the
rest come in short dresses like our Baby?" "Won't it
be lovely to see such a lot of new baby shoes?" "All
the Nurses will have to come, so it will be a Nurses'

party too!"   "What will the Babies get to eat?"
"Pap and arrow-root?"   "Wouldn't it be rich to ladle
boiled milk out of the big Punch bowl?"   "What entertainment for the Nurses?"   "Oh, pale ale and
brown stout!"   "Or else unlimited tea and toast!"
"Guess there'll have to be a supply of Mrs. Winslow's
soothing syrup!"   "Wonder if they'll all bring their
rattles?"   "Our Baby must have a coral to assist the
concert!"   "Ho! Baby! you're going to have a Ball!
a grand Baby Ball!   And all the fairy godmothers are
coming, and all the Baby Princesses, with rings on their
fingers and bells on their toes?"

Down came the authoritative gold thimble again to
quiet the confusion of tongues.

"That is not the kind of party at all that I want to
have," said the Young Mother.   "Now, girls, do be
still awhile till I tell you what my thought has been
about it.   We all know what a blessing our precious
Baby is; how we all love her, and what a pleasure she
is to us all—is she not?"

"Yes, indeed," rang out the Aunties, "she's just a
dimpled angel and worth her weight in gold!"

"Then," continued the Young Mother, speaking very

softly and tenderly, "it seems to me so selfish to keep all the happiness of her to ourselves, when we might make her the source of sweetness and enjoyment to others. Now, you know, girls, that rich people's children get and have everything—our Baby couldn't do much for them; it isn't to the happy infants who have corals and rattles, arrow-root and pap in plenty, that I want to give my Baby's party, but for the poor little creatures that never have heard a rattle or saw a bowl of good boiled milk in their short lives. Oh, ever since my Baby was born there has come up to me so often the cry of the children—the children who are not sheltered and cared for as mine is; and I have wept over the mothers who must weep over their little ones, because they have so little to give them in a world that must be so hard to them! Can we do nothing for these? Can we not give these babies a party, and make it an occasion of kindness and rejoicing?"

The Young Aunties were silent now, and most of the bright eyes were moist with the dew of feeling; their impressionable hearts and fancies had gone out to those other babies so different in all their surroundings from their own family pet. But one of the gay young girls—partly because she did not like the unusual sensation of gravity which had settled upon her sunny spirits, and partly from a naturally practical as well as fastidious turn of mind—suddenly exclaimed :

"But poor people's babies always smell so badly, and are so dreadfully dirty ! they are so sour and slobbery, and generally wear yellow flannel petticoats ! "

"Ah, dear ! " answered the Young Mother, "how can they be nice and sweet as our Baby, when the parents have to toil so hard, so early and so late, that there is hardly time to make the merest necessaries of life ? Besides, you must remember that there are some mothers so poor that they cannot afford even to buy soap ! "

"Oh, Sister, soap is so cheap ! " cried the practical Young Auntie.

"Yes—to us. But to them bread is so dear, and bread is the necessity and soap the luxury."

The practical Young Auntie was practical no longer; to be too poor to procure soap was a depth of distress to which her imagination had never descended. She had an immediate vision of a rich soap-boiler whose advances she had always scorned, but who loomed up now in her mind as a possible universal benefactor ; and in a momentary fancy she was herself standing at the door of his factory, dispensing bars of soap to a dirty crowd, as nuns deal out food to the beggars at the gate of a convent, and somehow the Soap-boiler did not seem so low down in the social scale of humanity as before; he became instead a kind of apostle to redeem the Great Unwashed.

Her passing reverie was interrupted by the Young Mother's voice, as she continued : "Dön't you think we could contrive at our party to provide these poor babies with some of the necessaries that their mothers have so much trouble to obtain for them, and that, perhaps, will leave them a little of their hard-earned money for other things ? "

"Soap, for instance," said the Young Auntie, who had scarcely got away from the Soap-boiler and his factory door.

The generous hearts of the Young Aunties were stirred, and the consultation was long and deep; and the girls went out of Baby's home with a thoughtful pucker in each smooth forehead, occasioned by profound consideration of each one's share in the new

6*

enterprise, and with much eager talk of the ways and means, and all they meant to do.

And lo! as the practical Young Auntie wended her way homeward, by a strange coincidence whom should she meet, face to face, but the Soap-boiler himself! and with a vague intention of securing future soap for scented babies, she absolutely allowed herself to return his respectful bow with a pleasant nod, whereupon the audacious Soap-boiler, who had hitherto secretly admired her afar off, took the liberty of joining her fair highness upon the open street. Once this man who thus dared would have been met with haughtiness and silence, and would soon have been made to feel that he was no fit escort for an aristocratic Young Auntie, albeit he had all the seeming of a presentable and courteous gentleman; but somehow, in the last hour soap had taken on a new dignity, and its manufacturer did not seem so near to the scum of the earth as before. So, involuntarily she was almost gracious, and was surprised to find that the despised individual was well educated, had refined tastes, and even some beautiful enthusiasms; and in her astonishment and humility at having so under-estimated a human soul because of a worldly business, she actually invited the Soap-boiler to Baby's party. Afterwards she felt half ashamed of it, and laughed ironically to herself as she pictured him entering in the midst of assembled babies, dragging in a great box full of brown soap. And at last it tormented her so that she had asked him, that she began to dream about him, and her nights were haunted by saponaceous visions until she almost began to envy those to whom soap was a luxury.

Soon the deft fingers of the Young Aunties began to fly in preparation; bundles of bright zephyrs adorned their tables; balls of worsted were forever being pounced upon by sportive kittens; odds and ends of yarn strewed each familiar place; every admirer was called upon to hold entangling skeins; and all their lighter talk was interspersed with grave counting of stitches, till it might have been thought that each one was weaving a Penelope's web, which was never to be finished. And they pursued the Grandfathers for coin to purchase Shetland wool, and tormented them perpetually for contributions to knitting-needles, till the Grandfathers—who, however, paid out on every demand, and were always rewarded by a kiss from rosy lips—

grumbled after the fashion of men when their pockets are touched, growled greatly over the "nonsense of it all," and declared that " babies were a nuisance anyhow!" and that "our Baby was too much spoiled!" at all of which the Young Aunties chaffed and coaxed, and came off triumphant. But the hearty Grandmothers entered into the spirit of the thing with real good-will, and gave excellent service in the cause. And the Poor Relation sent her small donation, neat and pure and simple as herself, and the Crippled Sister wrought night and day as she could, at her share of the sweet work.

And so came on the day of Baby's party, a day when the sun was shining and warm hearts were glowing; when Baby's home was made bright with flowers, and in the midst thereof stood a great basket, heaped up to overflowing with all kinds of warm and useful and pretty baby garments. Baby herself was dressed in her first short frock, much to her own intense delight, as she could thus uninterruptedly play with her disclosed feet, for the first time covered with the wee-est pair of colored slippers, which her round eyes contemplated with curious observation, and her chubby fingers began immediately to try and pull off. Never yet had she beheld anything so fascinating; and to kick the small phenomena back and forth, and crow with self-appro-bation, seemed to have become her crowning satisfac-tion.

The first to arrive were the Grandfathers and Grand-mothers, the latter each carrying a bundle of last con-tributions, and the former, half-laughing and half-grum-bling, protesting that the whole thing was an absurdity; that there were enough paupers in the world, without encouraging poor folks to bring any more into existence; that women, anyhow, always had more sentimen-tality than common sense; that because there was one Baby in the family, there was no reason to go mad over a whole lot of other babies! But the wary Young Mother held her little one up for them to kiss, and that stopped their further speech, for they immediately began to amuse and entice the infant with the gold heads of their canes, and straightway became as foolish over Baby as any woman belonging to them.

Then came in the Young Aunties, one or two at a time, in the prettiest of simple toilettes, and with the sweetest of youthful, happy faces all aglow with the ex-citement of benevolence, and all eagerness and excla-

mations over Baby's loveliness in its new attire; and
with one Young Auntie entered the undaunted Soap-
boiler, who had waylaid her on the road under the
pretence that he felt rather shy at going alone to a
party where he knew so few—much to her dismay, as
she had over and over again repented the momentary
enthusiasm of humanity which caused her to give the
invitation, and had hoped that he had forgotten it;
but somehow, as she crossed the threshold with him,
blushing with an unsubdued caste pride or shame, she
could not help but watch very narrowly the reception
accorded him, and her light heart was greatly relieved
to see that he was warmly greeted by the Grandfathers,
who, being sensible men of the world, thought a good
deal more of a man's character than his business; that
he was cordially welcomed by the Young Father and
Mother, whose sense of hospitality did not permit them
to exhibit any surprise, or any other feeling than pleasure, at his presence; and above all, that the other
Young Aunties sufficiently concealed their amazement
and scorn under the mask of distant courtesy; but
because she did perceive, notwithstanding, that in
their innermost hearts they were looking down on her

escort, her own rose up in involuntary championship, and made her so gracious and respectful to him that he enthroned her Queen of his Life forever.

Then the pure presence of the Poor Relation entered like a blessing in their midst, and there was a softness and tenderness in every one's manner as she moved from one to another in salutation, which showed that angels are not always entertained unaware.

And at last, hearty and cheery, with her big black coal-scuttle bonnet tied under her double chin, and in one hand the inevitable cotton umbrella—stout in the stick and faded in the stuff—while the other grasped the bulging basket whose lid was tightly secured with green ribbons, in rolled the Fat Nurse, who, still panting and blowing, having been settled on a wide seat with Baby trotting away on one knee, proceeded dexterously to open with a single hand that mysterious basket without which she was never known to appear, and about whose contents there had always been more or less curiosity ; and behold, when the lid was uplifted, there was the capacious interior filled to the brim with carefully packed sucking-bottles, while the mellow voice poured out an explanation : " You see, when this

ere precious Baby sent me an invite to come to the party
—cos, perhaps, I might help some of the poor mothers
with my experience—thinks I to myself, now I'd
like to do something for them poor little mites as don't
get much nussin', nor any too much vittles or comfort ;
but I have them belongin' to me as I have to take care
of, and so have mighty little money to indulge my feelings with, and I lay awake two or three nights off and
on a-cogitatin' and ruminatin' how I should make it out,
and at last I just set out mornin' after mornin' with
that basket of mine, and went to every house where I
had nussed, and asked the ladies to give me all the bot-
les they had done with for poor women as couldn't buy
'em ; but I didn't get enough, as babies keep comin' on
in most families, and bottles, like the long clothes, are
apt to descend to the next; so I went around every
place where I could find a lot of bottles that could be
made to do, and fixed 'em up with tops as don't cost
much, you know, and there they are, and welcome ! "

The Young Aunties told her that she was " a real,
dear, good old soul ! " and the Grandmothers patted her
on the shoulder and praised her good sense, while to
the glistening sight of the Poor Relation these plain

bottles sparkled like diamonds; but the Young Mother, thanking her warmly, brought the moisture to the small, twinkling eyes half buried in the fat cheeks, by stooping over and tenderly kissing the coarse, good-humored mouth, for though the Fat Nurse was homely, common, and ungrammatical, though she wore a frilled cap and a bombazine coal-scuttle, and carried a faded cotton umbrella, and though her "profession" was not the most exalted walk in life, still this Young Mother saw under all this the kind and generous heart, and only felt that "by their fruits ye shall know them!" And lo! at last, when they were thus gathered together, and waiting for the babies, the primmest of footmen, in the trimmest of livery, delivered with careful precision a very large package and a very short note, and all the assembled group were quite struck dumb to think that it had never entered any of their minds to ask Aunt Hannah; for the unexpected missive simply said; "As you have forgotten to invite me to the Baby's party, I send, by bearer, my contribution to the same, hoping it may be found useful and acceptable." The Young Aunties immediately thought of that grim fairy of the story-books who is always left out

at the christening, and comes in at the last moment,
furious at the slight, to counteract all the good gifts of
the other fairy godmothers. But though their Aunt
Hannah seemed a very grim fairy indeed to the Young
Aunties, there was nothing malicious in her gift; for,
when the package was opened, there lay a score of
violet and dove-colored merino Babies' cloaks, warm
and wadded, suitable and plain; and as they all stood
in a group looking at these there came a fresh tenderness into the face of one of the Grandfathers.

"We let Hannah too much alone," he softly said at
length. "Poor thing! she never forgets;" and then
noticing the curious looks on the Young Aunties' countenances, he added: "Ah! girls, Aunt Hannah is
homely and old now, but she was once as young and
pretty and happy as any of you. My sister had a great
sorrow long ago, and these little things tell me that she
has never forgotten. We must all go and see her
more. Her life must be lonely enough in her big,
empty house. Go and see her, girls—go and see your
Aunt Hannah!" And as he turned away there were
tears standing in the eyes that had just looked into the
past.

And hardly had the cloaks been laid out of sight when mothers and babies commenced to arrive. It was a pathetic sight to see them all collected together. All were scrupulously clean, in spite of the Young Auntie's foreboding, and some of the infantile faces fairly shone as if they had been well rubbed into unusual whiteness; and though there were indeed a few yellow flannel petticoats, these obnoxious garments had at least no shadow of dirt on them, while the poor dresses of the mothers were mended and washed and made as decent as possible, for it was a very rare holiday, and all seemed to have striven to be in everything becoming. The babies themselves were many of them scrawny and pale and miserable to behold, but not particularly noisy, for the silent patience of endurance enters early into the spirits of the very poor, and their occasional cries of want and pain were more of feeble whines than the healthy roar of indulged infancy. It stirred the hearts of the women to notice how lean and bony some of the tiny arms were, and how pinched and old a few of the little faces; but still some were round and rosy and lusty—evidences of Nature's success in spite of circumstances, and with sound lungs, which, however, they were much too interested in the novel scene to use.

There was thin and tired-looking Mary Maloney, who took in washing, and whose equally lean baby had never known any other cradle than a broken wash-tub, and who, when no kindly neighbor took care of her child during her absence, carried her washes home on one arm, and her baby on the other. And there was a consumptive seamstress, whose weird and unnaturally quiet infant looked like a little shrivelled up old monkey, with preternaturally keen and cunning eyes; and big, bouncing Kitty Flanagan, with a heart as ample as her broad bosom, on which reposed too sickly twins, the legacy of a dead daughter, and which tremendous charge the generous soul had accepted with a resignation which was almost cheerfulness, though she had to work almost day and night to keep the life in them, and some besides who were dependent upon her. And there were many others gathered in from the byways and hedges of life, and to whom need and sorrow were all too familiar, and pleasure a luxury they had scarcely ever known; so that in all these hard lives, so worn, so weary with toil and care, so unlovely and unbright·

ened, this sweet occasion of Baby's party became the
Day of Days. After the bustle of reception was over,
and all were comfortably seated around the parlor, the
Young Mother moved a small table in the midst, on
which was laid the large new Family Bible, which had
been one of her wedding presents, and on the blank
leaves of which between the Testaments the only records
were her own marriage and that of Baby's birth. She
read, half shyly and with tender grace, the beautiful
story of the Star of Bethlehem; and when she paused,
some of these poor mothers, who perhaps had never
even heard a line of the Good Book before, felt as if a
new sacredness had fallen on their own babies, since a
little child had once been worshipped by the Wise Men
of the East. Then she turned the cherished pages a
little farther on, and again read only three verses, the
three most beautiful verses that ever touched the universal heart of humanity; and it seemed to all those
untutored natures, who through all the burden of maternity had felt the throb of love, that this blessed voice
which, eighteen hundred years before, had rebuked the
disciples, still spoke to each one of them, and bade
them "Suffer little children to come unto me, and for-

bid them not," and because "of such is the kingdom of heaven," there fell the holiness of possible angel-hood upon each unseemly waif, and for a space there was a reverend silence as if the hands of Christ were in reality being laid upon the little ones, and even the babies themselves kept wonderfully quiet. Then one of the Young Aunties rose up and went to the piano, and sang this sweet benediction of children :

"To Thee, O God! whose face
    Their angels still behold,
We bring these children, that Thy grace
    May keep, Thine arms enfold.

"And as the blessing falls
    Upon each youthful brow,
Thy holy spirit grant, O Lord!
    To keep them pure as now."

And the hearts of the mothers were so full that tears fell down on the wan faces of the. babies; and then all the Young Aunties gathered together around the instrument, and chanted, in their clear, fresh tones, "The Mother's Hymn," that our honored Bryant wrote out of his poet's wisdom and insight; and the unfamiliar light and glow upon their mothers' counte-

nances, made them so strange to their babies, that they
raised up their voices also and wept aloud. Then the
doors were thrown open, and in was borne, not only
one punch-bowl of boiled milk, but another, borrowed
from the Grandmothers, brimming over with arrow-
root pap; and there was great frolic and fun among
the busy Young Aunties filling up the Fat Nurse's
acceptable bottles, and soon a gentle gurgling sound
proclaimed that the whole assembly were ecstatically
at peace; while the Fat Nurse sat in the midst, beaming all over with delight at the appropriateness and
usefulness of her present, and dealing out advice here
and there, after the decided fashion of one having
authority.

"You needn't tell me, Mrs. Maloney, that if that
child of yours had such feedin' every day it would
ever get plump and healthy! It ain't vittles it wants
so much as air! Yes, air! Don't I know well enough
how you folks shut yourselves up in your room, and
patch up every crack and cranny to keep out a
draught? Ain't you afraid as death of a shiver, and
keep every window down for fear of a bit of chilliness?
You think close air is warm air. Now,. if you'd put

any sort of a cover over your baby, and then fling up
your sashes, and let in the blessed breezes till the smell
and the mustiness were all cleared out, and there was
a chance to breathe something that you couldn't cut
with a knife, your child would gain a little flesh and
color, and you too for that matter! You're just killing
your baby with foul air; that's all that ails it; and it's
a good deal better to be a trifle cold than to be dyin'
by inches! Well, I know, my dear soul, that coal *is*
dear, and every one can't afford a fire; but a little of
the Lord's good, fresh air to sweeten your home won't
freeze you to death!" And then she unhesitatingly
accused another conscious mother of giving her baby
paregoric to make it sleep at night, or while she was
at work, as it was easy to be seen that the small creature was one of the restless, nervous sort who are
always teething and always crying. No denial or
excuse could deceive that practiced eye; but instead of
a severe and indignant protest, she imparted a piece
of information: "Don't you know what a sugar-tag is?
You just take a cracker and pound it up—crackers
don't cost as much as paregoric, and one will do two or
three times—and sweeten it a little, and tie it up tight

in a bit of rag; stick it into your baby's mouth, and it will suck away at it, and keep still for hours; try that, and throw your paregoric bottle away anyhow; for cryin' is natural, but stupor ain't."

And while she delivered her oracular injunctions, the Young Aunties were amused to notice that the Soap-boiler, sitting quietly near by, listened to her quite attentively, as though he thought the Fat Nurse was a character; who knew what she was about, and was well worth hearing; and she, nothing daunted by her unusual audience, gave these ignorant mothers, in a . few moments, more instruction on the proper physical rearing of their children, than perhaps they had ever learned in all their lives before.

Soon after, when the Babies were all inwardly refreshed, and many of them asleep, all the cushions and pillows in the house were brought into requisition, and all the sofas and arm-chairs were filled, and the Fat Nurse, Baby's own nurse, the two Grandmothers, and the Poor Relation were left to mind them all, while the mothers were ushered into the dining-room, where a plentiful repast had been prepared. The Young Mother had brought out all her prettiest china and finest glass, and

7

her table was set and garnished as though her guests were
the best of her friends; and the Grandfathers sat at
either end and carved for the hungry eaters till their
faces glowed with the exercise; and the Young Father
and Mother, the Young Aunties and the Soap-boiler
waited on them, and the latter acquitted himself so gracefully, was so thoughtful and considerate, and so gentle
and courteous to each poor woman as though she had
been the highest lady in the land, that one Young Auntie
in particular, watching him critically, began to think him
the noblest and truest gentleman she ever saw, and remembered the old story of Gareth, who served in the
palace kitchen for a year and a day before he proved
himself one of the gallantest knights of King Arthur's
Round Table.

After they had returned to the parlor, and each
mother was gathering up her own offspring, the Young
Mother noticed the Grandfathers standing together and
looking on. Directly they said a few words to each
other, and then suddenly disappeared; and amid the
greater freedom of chatter which had begun, she heard
their gold-headed canes striking the hall-floor, and the
front door closing behind them. For half an instant

she was mortified, but then reflected that there must be something more than weariness and disgust behind their departure, and she felt confident that in a little while they would be back again, as they had not spoken to her before going out.

Then the Young Aunties struck up a gay song with a well-known chorus, in which most joined, and then another and another, and when the laughter and noise became a little more than decorous, the great basket was borne in all heaped up with gifts. Everything that mothers could desire for their babies was there. Warm things, soft things, woollen things, fleecy things, knit things, and woven things, and even a rattle apiece for every baby present; and the Young Mother and Young Aunties had great joy in the delivery, first placing each article in Baby's tiny hands, to be given by her to each other baby, so that everything should be considered as Baby's own gift to the little ones.

The pleasure and gratitude of the mothers was pathetic to observe. Some were loud in their thanks, but some could hardly speak at all; and one of these, dumb with too much feeling, sank upon her knees and kissed the Young Mother's bountiful hands. But the climax was reached when Aunt Hannah's cloaks were brought forward and dealt out. Hardly, in their wildest dreams had these poor women hoped to ever have anything for their infants so dainty and comfortable; and when they were told that these had been sent to them by a lonely old lady who had no children of her own, the mother-souls vented themselves in all manner of quaint and tender blessings and good wishes for her whose generous heart had thus, amid her solitude, remembered the children of the poor.

Then every baby was invested with its new garments, submitting to the operation with unusual serenity, as if they too were charmed with their acceptable possessions; and in truth, the appearance of many was so improved by these pretty and bright additions to their scant attire, that the mothers were quite elated with pride, and grew eloquent in their praise of each fresh article.

And when the bustle of admiration had a little subsided, Kitty Flanagan, with the twins pressed to her ample bosom, decked in their new array and each enveloped in one of Aunt Hannah's cloaks, arose, and begged to be allowed to make a few remarks; and when a surprised silence was thus secured, she said right out of her full heart:

"Shure, and it's not meself that often shpakes out before my betthers; but it would be too mane to thim that has thrated us so splindidly if there was niver a one to say a word for the rist; and troth, I am just shure that I expriss the sintiment of ivery mother prisent when I wish that all the saints may guard the swate Baby as gave this party; and may the blissing of the Lord God Almighty and the love of the Virgin Mary be upon this house and all thim that's in it!" and she extended the twins, one on each arm, and waved them as if in benediction, and sat down with a very red face, while all the mothers cried "Amen!"

There was a little awkward pause of emotion; the mouth of the Young Mother quivered; the Young Aunties' eyes were very moist, and those of the Poor Relation shone as with a light; the Grandmothers coughed, and the Soap-boiler turned suddenly and looked out of the window, while the Young Father shook as much of Kitty Flanagan's hand as could be released from her hold of the twins.

And lo! when the time came for departure, there on

either side of the parlor door stood a bareheaded
Grandfather, each with a roll of crisp bank-notes in his
hand; and as every woman passed out one of these was
put in her hand with a " God bless you! " or "Good luck
to you! " by these sly old Grandfathers alternately—who
had slipped away to the bank together, at the time the
Young Mother was so sorry to see them leave the house,
in order to secure this pile of bright, clean bills, and be
back again to bestow them thus at the moment of departure; and when the last mother and baby had disappeared through the door, the Young Mother and all
the Young Aunties fell upon them, and kissed them
over and over for being such " precious, good old darlings! "

And everybody said that Baby's party had been a
grand success, and there was that sweet glow of happiness in the heart of each that came to them inasmuch
as they had done it to the least of these, His little ones;
and the Poor Relation remembered that when Simon
Peter answered to Jesus, " Yea, Lord, thou knowest
that I love thee," He said unto him, " Feed my
Lambs."

After this the audacious Soap-boiler became more

and more attentive to one particular Young Auntie,
who slowly and reluctantly, but involuntarily yielded
to his advances, much to the astonishment and amusement of the other Young Aunties, who watched the
afiair with much satirical interest, and chaffed her un-
mercifully, after the fashion of thoughtless girls who
did not care to see anything serious behind the mirth
of a good joke. One day she would find a cake of
fancy soap upon her toilette table, with the compliments of the Soap-boiler directed in the unmistakable
handwriting of a mischievous Young Auntie; another
time she would find her own soap spirited away from
its dish, and the address of the factory left in its place;
and sometimes small bouquets ingeniously cut out of
variegated soap would be surreptitiously arranged
around her room; and the very name of soap began to
be such a torture to this perplexed Young Auntie that
she blushed at its very mention; until one day the Fat
Nurse came in to say that there had just been left at
her house, for distribution among the poor mothers who
were at Baby's party, a dozen barrels of crackers and
as many more of sugar, "to help keep the babies
quiet," and an accompanying envelope full of orders

for coal, so that "the same babies might be kept warm
enough to get some pure air;" and in the midst of the
wondering who the generous donor could be, this
Young Auntie recollecting how attentively the Soap-
boiler had listened to the Fat Nurse's instructions to
the mothers on the day of Baby's party, felt, with a
great rush of tenderness, that it could have been only
he who had done this good thing, and her heart went
out to him to be his forever and forever. So that, when
she came into her room a day or two after, and saw a
caricature prominently placed over her mantel-piece
representing her admirer with a leather apron tied
around his waist, and a big stick in his hand stirring a
steaming kettle of soft-soap, and was aware of the
peeping faces of the assembled Young Aunties watching through the crack of the door the effect of their
latest attempt at ridicule, she indignantly tore down
the picture, rent it into shreds and stamped on them,
and then flinging wide the door, cried out in her anger
and anguish, "That it was a mean shame to vilify a
noble gentleman; that they knew as well as she did,
that though he owned the factory he did no such work
there; that he had inherited his business from his

father, and whatever they might think of it, had made
it by his honorable dealing the peer of any other; that
he was a good man and true, and that—that—they
might say what they pleased about it, but she loved
him—oh, she loved him!"

There was no more chaff after that. The Young
Aunties were all conscience-smitten immediately; they
rushed into the room; they put their arms around
her, and caressed her and cried over her; said they
were only in fun, and begged her to forgive them; and
praised the Soap-boiler with an affectionate hypocrisy
that brought her soul content; though they were very
much surprised to find that the Grandfathers were
mightily pleased with the match, on account of the
good name and great uprightness of the suitor's
character.

And on the day of the wedding, in fidelity to the
apostleship of cleanliness and appreciation of soap, a
large box of the same was left at the home of each
poor mother, who, at first, perhaps did not connect this
unexpected and remarkable gift with the gay Young
Auntie who had helped to make them all so happy on
that memorable day of Baby's Party.

7*

VII.

THE Poor Relation's Aged Father and Mother sat together in the vine-wreathed porch, in the glowing sunset of a mellow Autumn day. The sky was all glorious with purple and gold; roseate clouds, fringed with their silver linings, floated like islands of the blest upon an amber sea; while piled up against the wide horizon were the transparent pinnacles and lustrous domes of an ethereal temple with gates of pearl guarded by white-winged angels; and just overhead spread the tender, melting blue, with its unutterable calm that soothes the soaring spirit with the peace of God which passeth understanding. And the leaves on the vines seemed to have caught the changing colors of the heavens, and had turned crimson and yellow, and on every light breeze some of them were shaken down upon the earth. With the Aged Father and Mother, too, the Sunset of Life was coming on apace, and, like the fading leaves, they also were passing away. And as the old man sat with his hands clasped on the top of his staff, and looked out with his dim eyes towards the iridescent West, its glow seemed to wrap them about with lingering warmth, and to make the needles shine as they clicked through the Aged Mother's knitting. They had been silent for a while, each thinking the thoughts that come to the very old—of a past full of memories, of a future so short in this world, so tinged with mingled feelings as it extended into the next.

"Wife," at length said the old man, "we, too, are going down—going down like the sun ; we have borne the burden and heat of the day, and the shades of evening are gathering fast ; .we have had a hard life together ; will you be sorry when the night comes on, and there is no more any work or device in the grave ?"

"Not sorry, Father," she answered, with the sweet quavers of age in her mild voice, "for the grave is such a precious rest for these worn-out bodies ; there will be no more aches or weariness there, and it is pleasant to think that for the part of us which is not body there is the Beyond, where one likes to believe there are no more tears. And, Father, if our lives have been hard in some respects, it has been very happy in others; surely it has been a great blessing that we have been spared to each other, that we have had all our good and ill together; and then, above all, there were the children!"

"The children!" replied the old man, a little bitterly, "were there ever children born into this world that were not a disappointment in some way or other to their parents?"

"Oh, not all, not all!" answered the Aged Mother. "Think of our Mary and her Crippled Sister!"

"Ay, ay," said the Aged Father, "they are good enough—true and tender; but then the lives they have had! All sorrow, and pain, and labor! It has been an ever-piercing thorn in my side that our girls could not have been sheltered in from every hardship and every grief—that they should not have had happy homes and little ones of their own, like that Baby who was here to-day! And it might have been—it all might have been, if it had not been for the wickedness of that boy!"

"Oh, Father, Father! don't say hard things of him,

for it was not wilful wickedness, only the folly and wildness of youth; and I am sure, if he had lived, he would have atoned long ago. Remember only that he was our first child—our eldest son!"

"I remember it only too well!" sternly replied the old man. "I remember my joy when he was born; what high hopes I built on him; how I worked for him, and watched his growth with such pride and gladness! I tell you, wife, that the love with which a father loves his eldest son passes the love of a woman, for he sees in him a fresher, newer self, and the embodiment of his race, and there is a sort of sadness and yearning in it, too, from his own knowledge of life; and I loved this son so, and tried to make him strong and wise. And after all, he dragged my name in the dust, and ruined us all over there in the Great City. I have never been the same man since."

"But oh, Father!" and the clicking needles were silent, and fell into her lap, as she laid her withered hand on her husband's arm, and there was a sob amid the pleading tones; "think how heart-struck he must have been when he took his own life rather than face your wrath; think what an agony of suffering and shame our

boy must have gone through when he could thus plunge
into death to escape it!   Oh, don't say it was cowardly,
Father, for he was not himself when he did it!   He
was insane with remorse, for our John had been such a
brave boy!" and the two wrinkled hands were wrung
together, and a tear flashed down upon the bright needles.   The old man put his arm around the trembling
form, and gently answered: "You are right, Mother
dear; and it is not well for me to go back to that sad
time, or to set a single act of temptation and wrong-
doing against all the other years of affection and obedi-
ence.   And after all, we had great comfort in our
grave, steady Jamie!"

"But oh!" said the Aged Mother, all stirred up with
these reminiscences, "it was hard, too, that he should
have died in a foreign land, away from us all, and with
only strangers to close his eyes!"

And a new shadow fell over the old man's face; the
Aged Mother saw it, and her quivering arms went
round his neck, and she pressed her white and wrinkled
cheek against his wan face.

"Dear," she murmured, "it may seem a strange
thing, but I very rarely think of our boys as dead or

lost to us; mostly I look forward, and see them, radi-
ant and beautiful, in that other world where I am going
to meet them. Ah! Father, you will never be hard upon
our Johnnie there, for all things will be made known
to you then! and Jamie will be just your other self."

"Well, wife," answered the old man softly, "I believe it may be so, for, after all, John really loved us,
and by the love that was in him he may have been made
meet for heaven, and by love he shall be forgiven!".

The purple and gold of the setting sun flashed out
more gloriously than ever; the white pinnacles and
shining domes of the ethereal Temple grew more and
more luminous, and the tender blue above seemed to
drop down its inexpressible calm like the very dew
of heaven; the yellow autumn leaves floated awhile
on the soft breeze before they rested on the damp
mould, and a silence more eloquent than words fell
upon the Aged Father and Mother, as with clasped
hands they still looked out towards the glowing West.

Then the aged woman said softly out of her reverie
of remembrance: "Dear Father! you always think of
the children as grown up; but they always come back
to me, when I am alone, as little children still. Often

and often I sit by the nursery fire in our old home, and
they come in with their pattering feet, and group themselves about me in the twilight: Johnnie, with his curly
head upon my knee; Jamie, always grave and steady,
on his cricket in a corner of the hearth; our dear
Mary, with the flames lighting up her golden hair and
angel face; our poor, afflicted one, bright and restless
then, dancing round me on her tiny feet; and the baby
—oh, Father! the baby that never grew up, lying close
upon my happy breast! See! I have only to close my
eyes, and they are all there. I forget Johnnie's sin,
and Jamie's far-away grave; I forget our Mary's toil-
ing, lonely life, and the pains of her Crippled Sister; I
forget the tears I shed for my baby; for I only behold
the faces of their childhood—the innocent, sweet faces,
untouched by the world and unspoiled by time! They
come in and out to me all day long; I hear their young
voices; I feel their clinging arms! They have been
men and women, sinners and sufferers, but they are my
little children always still!"

"Ah! would we could have kept them so," replied
the old man, "kept them innocent and unstained, and
untried forever! for what do the years bring us all?

And if all things had turned out well, in the course of nature and time our children would probably have turned to other interests, and wrung our hearts anyhow by separation! As it is, what has life brought them, and what has it brought us? Death, and sorrow, and an old age of poverty and regrets!"

The Aged Mother clasped his hand firmly. "No, dear! no regrets for me. I have had my children; there is no regret for me in that—even about John; and in our deepest poverty I could always go back in my heart to our old home, and feel all the love-richness of my early motherhood. There is no poverty for a mother whose children have loved her! We cannot judge how life has dealt even with our own. How do we know but that Johnnie's sin may have been his salvation from worse, and that the Angel of Death may not have led him into some condition fitter for his nature? and if Jamie died, Jamie had lived well; there never can be any regrets about Jamie! and surely the lives of our Mary and her Crippled Sister are a daily lesson and blessing! And I have my baby in heaven—my baby that never has grown up through all these years! Father, we must have no regrets at God's dealings with us. A higher wisdom than ours ordereth all things right!" And the Aged Father bowed his head, and reverently said "Amen!"

The light in the sunset sky was something wonderful to see; the very splendor of the innermost heavens seemed to glow through its magnificence of color; the waves of the amber sea spread farther and farther, and the silver-fringed islands deepened in their roseate hue; the wings of the angels guarding the gates of pearl were too luminous for eyes to rest on; and the shining pinnacles and domes seemed to be wreathed with ascending flames; the measureless depths of the blue above were still calm with their unspeakable peace; and the dying leaves ceased for a little while to fall, but floated, floated softly still, as silence once more fell upon the Aged Father and Mother.

After a quiet space, the old man, with his dim eyes still looking outward towards the iridescent hues, said a little faintly, as the breeze lifted his snowy hair: "Wife, the days are very long; the sun is slow in going down; I am weary, and I would the end were come!"

And she answered gravely, "It cannot be far off,

for our work is done and the darkness is drawing near."

The purple and gold lost a little of their brightness; the waves of the amber sea waxed paler and withdrew from the far-off verges; the roseate islands paled to a delicate pink; over the lustrous domes and pinnacles of the ethereal temple a scarcely perceptible white mist seemed to arise; at the gates of pearl the angel wings lost something of their dazzling sheen, and in the lovely blue overhead a grayish shadow mingled with its brooding peace; more and more of the crimson and yellow leaves slipped away from the thinning vines, were whirled about faster in the cooler air, and dropped swiftly upon the waiting mould.

The old man turned his dim eyes from the fading West to gaze upon the wrinkled face of his life-long companion. "Dear," he said, "the night is dark and the grave is cold; but there is one thing that has never been dark to me, night or day—the light of your loving eyes; and one thing that has never been cold, even through the dreariest winter—the warmth of your wifely heart. God bless you, love of my youth and consoler of my age!"

And the worn old hand shook that caught hold of hers; the touch of it chilled her very life-blood, and a strange shadow passed over his aged face.

"Father, father!" she gasped out, as she leaned over with pallid lips to kiss his, already cold and white, "do not leave me alone! take me with you to the children!".

"Come!" he just whispered with the last fleeting breath; "we will go together to our children!" and the shadow that was on his face passed over to hers.

The faint gleam of the purple and gold died out; the fading flush of rosy isles paled and paled till even the silver lining lost its brightness; the glow of the amber sea was drawn inward from the gathering shades of evening that swept over it to the changing gates of pearl, where the angels' wings were soaring away in snowy, transparent clouds; while behind the dimming veil of mist the ethereal domes and pinnacles were dissolving like the baseless fabric of a vision; and over the peace of the heavenly blue the blackness of silent night was spreading fast. The crimson and yellow leaves had lost their color in the failing light, and lay an undistinguishable heap upon the dew-damp mould, while the last rays of the dying day lingered upon the staff which had fallen at the old man's feet, and upon the bright needles which would click in the busy fingers no more forever. And over the vine-wreathed porch the gray shadows of night crept about the Aged Father and Mother, who sat very still together with clasped hands when the Sunset of Life was over.

VIII.

AUNT HANNAH lived in a grim, gray mansion on the outskirts of the town, and to the gay Young Aunties, bright with their untried life and joyous with early hope, Aunt Hannah was a very grim and gray personage herself; for she resided alone in this large, empty house, full of the solid, heavy furniture of other days, keeping the casements always darkened, so that the rooms seemed haunted by gloomy shadows, and moving about therein with a grave, slow presence, as of one who carried a solemn weight. Nothing was ever awry in that silent house; the high-backed chairs stood straight against the wall in their accustomed places from year to year, and the big, old-fashioned bedsteads, with their canopies and draperies, were more like funeral catafalques than couches for the living. The primmest of footmen opened the hall-door to rare visitors with a subdued and sepulchral air, suggestive of an undertaker; and the fattest, laziest, nattiest of coach-men in antiquated coat and capes, drove the fat, lazy, shining old horses at a snail's pace when Aunt Hannah went in her roomy coach to make her annual duty call on her brother's family. Then the unwilling Young Aunties made expressive wry faces to each other on the stairs as they went down to endure her visit, and sat stiffly round the parlor, hammering their brains for stu- pid commonplaces with which to entertain her—with all their merry quips and quirks banished from their lips, and all their airy gossip laid aside as something too uncongenial for the chilling atmosphere of so severe a guest. Even the kindly Grandmother grew less cor-dial and more studiously polite with this reserved and solitary woman; and if the hearty Grandfather kissed his sister with warm welcoming, a tinge of sympathetic sadness seemed always to fall over him as he talked with her; and she, going not at all into the world, had but few subjects of conversation for them all, and it was with a great show of deference and stifled sighs of relief that their occasional intercourse terminated. And so Aunt Hannah dwelt apart in her grim and echoing house, a lonely woman little known. She manifested so little interest in the outer world, that it was only on family occasions that she was recalled or regarded as one of themselves. Possibly, if she had been poor and in want, the loving kindness of these kindred hearts would have drawn her among them, and shared more of their own life with her. But Aunt Hannah was extremely rich ; and while the worldly Grandmother sometimes thought of this with a spasmodic access of interest and attention, other members of the household seemed to make it an additional cause for distance. The Young Aunties had a vague understanding that some great sorrow had once made Aunt Hannah's days dark and dreary ; but they had so many light matters of their own to engage their hearts and time, that they troubled their minds and memories very little with one they scarcely sought.

But the Young Mother's spirit was stirred within her by the present of little cloaks which Aunt Hannah had sent to Baby's Party ; and an unusual interest had been excited when Grandfather No. One had spoken with so much emotion of the forgotten fairy who had not been bidden to the festivity. She pondered these things in her heart of hearts, and her thoughts lingered about the grim, gray house and its grim, gray tenant. Surely, it seemed to her, that was a tender soul who had cared so considerately for the infants of the poor, and more and more she felt that in the woman's nature there must be sweet founts that might be reached by little hands; and there came over her a great yearning towards this unloved being, who, in her unremembered loneliness, had sent forth such a token of goodness to unknown babies. It occurred to her, that if the habitual barrier of reserve could be penetrated and the precious humanities within once aroused by some gentle ministry, that Aunt Hannah might be drawn out of her seclusion to be a power in the world and a benediction to others; and she was strongly moved to rise up and go to her with such greeting as should open the way to more familiar amenities. But the Young Mother was proud and delicate and quixotic as any uncalculating soul, and her cheek colored as she fancied that her motive might possibly be misunderstood; but a higher inspiration than that came upon her with the sudden pity that Aunt Hannah's very wealth should shut her away from the approaches of real affection. Still, it

8

was not an easy matter to get nearer to an interior nature through the ordinary method of formal visits, and the Young Mother, who had been a gay girl herself, had been frozen up like all the other Young Aunties by the undemonstrative demeanor; but at last the idea dawned on her that as Aunt Hannah must have a feeling for babies—or she never would have furnished those dainty cloaks—perhaps Baby might be the very best means by which to find her innermost heart. So Baby was forthwith arrayed in all her glory, and borne by Baby's Nurse to the door of the grim, gray house, where Baby's Young Mother took her in her own arms, and was admitted alone, by the primmest of footmen, to the silence of the solitary halls.

Amid the oppressive shadows of the gloomy parlor she sat waiting with a beating heart for the grim, gray woman, over whose threshold, she compassionately meditated, no other baby had ever come. Then slowly, stately, coldly, plain and pale, Aunt Hannah entered; and before she could scarcely recognize her visitor in the dim light, the Young Mother had gone swiftly forward to her, and kissed her over and over on her lips, her eyes, her brow. People rarely kissed Aunt

Hannah, and then not often with particular warmth, so that she was at once struck dumb with surprise.

Then the Young Mother spoke in her earnest, winning voice:

"Dear Aunt Hannah, I am very sure you must love babies, so I have brought mine to see you." And Baby, not a whit abashed by a stranger, put out her chubby arms, and cooed up into the new face as if she found nothing there to frighten, of grimness or of grayness; but a strange pallor spread over the worn countenance, and the Young Mother saw with dismay that her cold-mannered kinswoman had commenced to tremble as with a chill. But Baby put up one of her dimpled hands, and touched the faded cheek, and the next instant the little golden-ringed head was clasped close to a heaving breast. The Young Mother was too amazed to speak; she stood still a moment while the older woman mastered her unexpected emotion, for she instantly divined that the sight of her child had touched the chord of some passionate sorrow which had never died. But Aunt Hannah strove to assume her usual deportment, and to converse upon ordinary topics, though she never lifted her eyes off Baby's small figure,

and her lips quivered as she talked, till at last, as if the
fountains of the great deep broke up, all at once she
cried out suddenly, " A baby ! a baby ! In my arms !
on my heart ! "

" And why not ? " softly said the Young Mother,
" they are a woman's arms; it is a woman's heart ! "
And Aunt Hannah looked at her as if half frightened
at having betrayed her feelings, and half timidly, as
if she scarcely expected to be believed. " Dear," she
said, " it must surprise you that I, of all people, should
be so agitated at seeing your little one ; but, do you
know, it is the first time in all my life I ever held a
baby in my arms ? "

The Young Mother was almost shocked, knowing
how often babies are more plentiful in the world than
arms to hold them ; but then it was Aunt Hannah, and
Aunt Hannah had lived shut up from the world, babies
included, this many a long year. " Dear Auntie," she
answered, " perhaps I have disturbed you too much by
bringing baby to you; but you see, we all think so
much of our blessing that I could not bear that there
should be one member of the family who did not know
her, and I wanted you to love our darling too." And

Aunt Hannah answered her slowly and sadly, " It is a long time since I loved anything!"

The Young Mother laid her soft hand on the one that still clung to her child, and the elder woman broke out in quicker words: " I thought I should never love anything in this life again; and now you have brought me a baby—of all things to *me*, a baby! and it is stirring the old life in my heart once more!" and she drew the Young Mother close down to her, and whispered, half gasping, as if each syllable came forth with a wrench of pain: "Don't you know—have you never heard—that I too was once a mother?" " No, Auntie," answered the Young Mother, " I did not know that; and some day, dear, when you have come to love my Baby, will you tell me about yours?" and Aunt Hannah drew her closer, closer, whispering still, as if she could not breathe aloud the secret sorrow of her soul : " Yes, I was once a mother, but I never had a baby!" and then answering the puzzled look which crossed the Young Mother's face, she added, with a great sob, " Oh, child! my baby died before it was born." And then the Young Mother understood that this disappointed hope had been the overflowing drop of despair in Aunt Hannah's bitter cup. What could she say to such a life-cherished grief, that had been a matter of so little moment in the family that it had been forgotten, or never spoken about, and yet which had helped to darken and make solitary this sad woman's whole existence. She laid her fair cheek against the worn face. "Dear, dear Auntie," she said, "I can imagine how hard that was! To the mother-heart our child is always our child, and the greatness of the loss is not to be measured by the life!" Aunt Hannah clung to her, held her tight, and the arms of both women were around the Baby.

"Child, child," she murmured, "for thirty years I have not spoken of this; I never, never could speak of it before; my heart was broken then, for I lost all at once—all at once! Come with me," she said, starting up, "I must tell you all now, for you are a woman and a mother, and you will understand. Your Baby's hands have torn away the seal of my silence!" And with Baby making unresisted clutches at her brooch, she kept her in her arms as she walked up the broad staircase, followed by the Young Mother with her soul full of wonder and sympathy. She led the way through dimly-lighted passages and shaded rooms, to one which at a first glance the Young Mother saw had been arranged as a nursery ; for there was a costly cradle in a corner, covered with faded silk and rich lace grown yellow with time ; and there was the dainty baby's basket, with the same color paled away by the years, and a coral and bells lying on the bureau in whose drawers she surmised there were laid away the little garments that had never been worn ; and over the deep fireplace with its bright andirons, and piled-up un-lighted logs, there hung a man's portrait which seemed to look down still upon Aunt Hannah's plain and aging features with a young and loving face. And there the two women sat down together, and as Aunt Hannah poured out the story of her past to the Young Mother, Baby fell asleep with its tiny golden head nestled upon that bosom which had never before pil-lowed an infant's slumber.

"I was a very happy girl," she said, "not merry and gay as your bright young sisters very likely are among themselves, but rather grave and silent, and a little shy in my ways, but still truly and peacefully happy. You

know your father and I lost our parents when we were
children, but we grew up nevertheless under kindly
and careful guardianship, and there was not a cloud in
all the untroubled sky of my early years; and when
love came to me it was so gradual, so natural and so
sweet, that I never dreamed of the depth and intensity
of my own nature; and all things went so smoothly and
pleasantly for me as regards my marriage—for my husband was young, well-born, well thought of, and very
rich. And when he brought me home to this old house,
which had been his father's before him, and welcomed
me into its walls with a grace and earnestness as charming as it was precious, I lifted up my heart in wordless
thanksgiving as the most blessed among women. We
lived here two or three such happy, perfect years, that
if it had not been for the memory of them I never,
never could have borne the crushing weight of the
after-desolation. Two or three years, and I had but one
desire in the world. It seemed to me that a love so
entire, so mutual, ought to blossom out in the crowning
flower of a child that should be partly him and partly
me, as the very personation and consecrated consumma-
tion of our blended spirits. And at last my desire was

about to be fulfilled. Dear, I can hardly tell you, it was something so strange and so sacred, with what lofty and holy aspirations I was filled. To be the author of a living soul, the originator of an immortal being, the selected instrument in the miracle of creation! Oh, the mystery, the awe, the glory of it, filled me with humility, with ecstasy, with daily worship. What a new world of visions and hopes opened on me; what an overwhelming sense of responsibility overmastered me; what a going forth and clinging to the divine comforted me! All my faculties enlarged, my instincts widened. I became part of the whole beating pulse of humanity, since, in my exaltation, all humanity seemed also to be parent to my child. And there were times when the divinity of love so flooded my soul that I realized the emanation of all existence from the Fatherhood of God. I longed with inexpressible yearning that this coming being should be in all things pure and unblemished and beautiful; and I, who was no more myself to myself, or of any worth save as the mother of my child, I was minutely careful of my acts, my thoughts, even of my surroundings. I studied and strictly conformed to physiological laws; I read only the loftiest and noblest

8*

books ; I steadfastly put away from me every narrow
or unelevating sentiment; I lived, moved, and had my
being in an atmosphere of exquisite harmony, inspiring
pursuits, and delicious reveries.   I lived long future
years in my child's life ; I peopled this old house and
these silent rooms with other little shapes; I heard
their footsteps on the stairs, their voices in the halls.   I
even lived in my children's children ; and through it all
always was the beloved face of their Father beaming on
me, if possible, more tenderly as a Mother than a Wife.
And I loved him so.   I think only a woman can comprehend the added sense of belonging, the solemn reali-
zation of being really flesh of his flesh, bone of his bone,
of being truly joined together beyond any possible
chance of putting asunder, with which I loved my husband as the father of my child.   And loving him so,
living thus in my hopes and dreams, without a shadow
as large as a man's hand to warn me of the wrath to
come, I saw him go forth one day, strong in his youth,
full of health and happiness and love, and in a single
hour they had brought him home to me—quite dead!
He had been thrown from his horse, had struck his temple in the fall, and had been killed instantly.   After

that 1 remember nothing more. When my mind came back to me, I recollected that my baby ought to have been born, and my first looks searched for it and my first words asked for it. They told me, a little sadly, but as if they felt it was but a small calamity compared with the greater loss, that it had died before it was born. Its father's death had slain it. When they told me that, I answered never a word, but turned my face to the wall and laid there for days like a stone. And it seemed to me as if my heart had turned to stone within me. What could others know of my dead hopes, my buried visions? What understanding could any one else have that I was torn asunder, had lost flesh of my flesh, bone of my bone, was a mere nothing and part of being in becoming less than a wife and mother—a mere desolate self, the wreck of what was once a complete woman! So I never said much to any one. My sorrow was deeper than words, almost deeper than tears; and I took up my life again in a dull sort of way, never caring greatly for anything more, and have lived ever since alone with my dead. When I knew your Baby had been born, so near to me, my heart trembled towards it; and when I heard about your Baby's Party,

somehow a tender feeling towards those little waifs
came over me; and now that you have brought this little one here, see how the very sight and touch of a
baby has pierced the long repression, and opened up
the very secrets of my soul!"

With reverent and caressing hand the Young
Mother drew the drooping head upon her shoulder.
"Dearest Auntie," she said, "because I too am a
mother, I understand all of it—the joy, the aspiration,
the hope, the awful sorrow, and the life-long void.
And I know—I know there can never be any love like
the love you have lost on earth; but dear, dear Auntie!
if you will let us all come about you, you do not know
how tenderly we will all feel towards you, and what
a real pleasure it will be to every one of us to be with
you, to love you, to make your life a little less lonely.
It is not good for any one to be alone so much; and
with a heart so capable of loving, you would have more
comfort than you think in giving out feelings to others.
Dear Auntie, may I send Baby to you often, and bring
the girls round to cheer you up?"

Aunt Hannah sat silent a moment. "Child," at
length she answered, "there is so little in me to interest

you young people! I have lived shut up with my past
and my books so long that your world is like a strange
land to me; my ways are not your ways."

" You are our own dear Auntie," replied the Young
Mother, " and we are going to love you, and make you
love us just as you are. Only let your heart come out
to us, and we will try and bring you a little happiness
to brighten up this long gloom and solitude ! "

And Aunt Hannah had tears in her eyes and sobs in
her voice as she said : " Dear, you shall all come to me
if you will, for I have been lonelier than any one
knew, and I did not dare to let myself feel till this
minute how much I longed for other souls."

And after that the two women talked long together ;
talked much of the family, and a little more of the dead,
and naturally then upon that most universal of all subjects, the life beyond the grave, and the hope of meeting
again the loved ones who had gone before. And when
the Young Mother dwelt upon the beautiful faith, and
spoke to Aunt Hannah as if her lost baby was surely an
angel in the heavens, Aunt Hannah made sad reply :

" Ah! dear, how do I know? No sign has ever been
made me from the other side. And the best authorities

cannot tell whether a human being is really a soul till
the hour of its birth; and it is of souls we cherish our
dreams of immortality. All these long years I have
, beat against the blind wall of an ignorance that can
never be enlightened in this world. I have studied all
that has been written about it, and at last—at last, I
can only say, ' I do not know ! ' This thought of the
Beyond is with me always. To me my husband always
is—no reason destroys that faith; but about my baby
all is doubt! I think if I had seen its face I might
have had more sureness, and I have spent hours upon
hours trying to see with my heart how it might have
looked ; but it is always dim, shadowy, far off from me
—I cannot make it alive. I have lived in sorrow upon
the memory of a dream."

The Young Mother's heart was too full for speech.
Here was a new phase of grief for which she knew no
consolation ; for she was not wise in metaphysics, and
her simple trust had never known aught of those refine-
ments of casuistry with which brooding and solitude
torture searching intellects. Only the many, many
melancholy days and unhappy nights of this life-long
desolation rose up before her, and the sympathy of her

whole loving nature welled over to this stricken woman who could not even look out to the realms above and behold her baby's face as 't were the face of an angel.

After that there began a new life about Aunt Hannah. Baby went to her every day; and in Baby's Nurse she instinctively perceived that there too was one who had suffered, and there came to be a gentle ministry of unspoken interest between the two that brought healing to each. Then the Young Aunties began to drop in—a little shyly and very respectfully at first, but soon warming up into their natural selves as more constant companionship wore off reserve on both sides; the quips and quirks came back in her presence, and the airy gossip was no longer withheld. Aunt Hannah's heart was younger than she knew, for all her youth had only been buried under her sudden and nourished affliction, and began to bubble up again in familiar intercourse with youthful spirits; and soon the old house was seldom without one or other of these gay and merry girls. The Grandfathers walked round of evenings to chat with her, and even talked with her sometimes of stocks and markets and business ven-

tures, as one having many moneyed concerns, and said to
each other that "Hannah was not wanting in good,
sound sense." The hearty Grandmothers trotted in
and out on all sorts of errands, till Aunt Hannah was
almost bewildered by the multiplicity of interests
which dawned on her, and the deference with which
these kindly old ladies regarded her opinions and suggestions. But in truth the hearts of all these women
were touched to the core by the thought of that unused
cradle in the empty room ; and the remembrance of it
made them very gentle and earnest towards the lonely
woman. The Young Father and the Young Mother
seemed to think there was no one like her, and the
Poor Relation grew as dear to her as a sister. And
Aunt Hannah was fast learning that the love of kindred and the exchange of intimate affection was the
very sweetness of life itself.

And the solitary home commenced to blossom like a
rose. First one window and then another was opened,
till the glad sunlight filled every crack and cranny of the
once silent halls and gloomy rooms. Then one Young
Auntie and then another brought in a pot of flowers,
and the color and beauty were like a welcome surprise

where the shadows used to lurk, and in a little while all the sills were bright with blooms; and one day a blithe canary made the wondering walls ring with its echoing melody; and so came back life, and light, and music to the grim and gray old house.

And when a delicate pink tint settled on Aunt Hannah's faded cheek, and her eyes took to shining at the new order of things, the audacious Young Aunties never rested till they had arranged her hair in more modern style, and got her dress altered to the fashion of the day; and they rummaged through long-locked presses, and found rare old creamy laces and beautiful jewels, and took as much delight in decking her out with them as though they were children adorning a favorite doll; and then they danced around her in admiration, and marched her up to mirrors and bade her look how young and pretty she was growing, almost as pretty as the darling Baby herself—the Baby, who was the Young Aunties' highest standard of perfection; and wondered in their own hearts how they ever could have thought Aunt Hannah a grim and gray old woman; for love and companionship had freshened her face as well as her soul, and the strangeness and

the sweetness of being sought and petted and made
much of by these young people made her heart very
warm and soft towards them, so that she was as pliable
as wax in their hands, and they did nearly as they
pleased with her. And a quaint, hidden humor began.
to sparkle dryly up in her talk which struck out
answering fun from these merry girls, and so it came
about in time that Aunt Hannah felt that she gave as
much amusement as she shared.

Grandfather No. One was never tired of expressing
his joy at his sister's altered ways, and Grandfather No.
Two thought it was as good as a play ; the Grandmothers said it was a " resurrection ; " the Young
Father told his wife she was a magician, and the Young
Mother answered that it was the dear Baby who had
wrought the miracle ; but the Poor Relation, sitting in
the twilight with the Crippled Sister, said that " it was
all the goodness of God."

The primmest of footmen was driven distracted by
these remarkable changes, and was dimly conscious
that they had reached even to him, and that he himself was no longer quite the same either ; he had to
open the hall-door so often and answer so many cheer-

ful voices, that his own lost something of its sepulchral
tone, and with half a dozen gay young Aunties flying
in and out all day long, asking all sorts of questions and
giving all kinds of orders, it was impossible to maintain
the solemnity of an undertaker; gradually, under the
exactions of these busy spirits, the dignity of his office
relaxed, and he found himself doing ever so many
things that had no relation to his position as a footman,
and quite incompatible with continued primness. At
first, in the confidence of the lower regions, he was
inclined to resent the increase and alterations of his
functions, and said more than once that he "Couldn't
stay where there was so many goings on, though he
had lived with the Missus ever since he wore buttons."
But he never could get away from those Young
Aunties; at the first prim sign of insubordination delivered in the most sepulchral tones, his puzzled brain
was tormented with the wildest of chaff, and he retired
to the lower regions again in utter bewilderment as to
whether he was the most important or the most ridi-
culed footman that ever donned livery. Then the
plants and the bird seemed to afford him unusual interest, and he was observed to steal into the rooms and

take surreptitious sniffs at the flowers, while he almost surfeited the canary with furtive offerings of sugar. In a little while he actually took to smiling paternally on the pranks of the Young Aunties, and in the course of time became the abject slave of these arbitrary damsels.

The fat coachman, as he himself expressed it, "was just turned topsy-turvy; scarcely knew if he was on his head or his heels with so much going and coming; and the horses were a-getting thin with exercising, and the flesh was a-wearing off his own bones!"

"Jeems," he said to the prim footman in a confiden tial conference in the lower regions, "Jeems, they ain't nateral, these rum changes. When folkses have lived such a lot of years along all quiet and easy, why they can't keep on comfortable without stirring everybody up I'm blowed if I can see!"

"But, after all," replied James, "the changes are kinder pleasant when you get used to 'em; we'd got so set into being gruesome that we didn't know there was anything better in the world till the Missus' relations came round. I'm sure I pretty near a-yawned my head off many a night in this very room for want of something to think about!"

"Well, I guess you got it now," said the fat coachman, "for I ain't hardly got time to think at all between
'em all. But it's them gals as aggerawates me the
worst. They're as full of tricks as monkeys, and you
never know whether they're poking fun at you or not,
even when they gives you an order."

"Oh," answered James, in the warmth of his new
allegiance, "they're young and light-hearted; they
don't mean harm; and I'm sure there ain't many young
ladies as would be as free-spoken and cordial, even to
old servants like us. They've a nice way of making
you feel as if you were just as good as themselves, and
know you won't presume on it."

"Entirely too free-spoken for my idees," retorted the
fat coachman; "for half the time you don't know what
they're talking about; and there's one of 'em keeps
a-calling me out of my name all the while, as if it was
a joke, and a-proddin' at me about widders, as if I was
given to gallivanting round. 'Mr. Weller,' she says
to me, and she turns to the Missus, and says she, 'Now
Auntie, ain't he Mr. Weller out and out?' and the
Missus she smiles, first at her and then at me—and I
must say the Missus is a differing-looking woman since

she took to smiling—and she says, ' Mr. Weller is an invallable coachman!' And then the young un she looks at me with a long face, and says very solemn, ' But, Mr. Weller, you must beware of the widders!' 'I don't know none!' says I, getting red, for thinks I, ' maybe somebody's been telling lies about me!' 'Widders are dangerous, Mr. Weller,' she keeps on. 'Well, Miss,' says I, 'I ain't after no widders, and I ain't afeard o' none!' and the Missus she just laughs out, the first time I heard her laugh since she was like that same young un there, before the drefful time when they brought the Master home stiff and stark; and you know it kinder made me choke all up to hear her laugh again; and I makes my best bow, and says I, 'If you please, miss, I'll look out for widders, and I'll be Weller or anybody else, if it's going to make my Missus laugh like that!' and that there young un she just jumped up, and grabbed my hand, and shook it, and said she, ' You dear old Weller, if you ain't good enough to be the blessed Pickvick hisself!' There's another name she's got for me, and blow me if the whole of 'em ain't at it ever since, first one with their Weller and another with their Pickvick, and a-ordering

me to drive to the Markess of Granby, when they mean
the summer-house on the hill, and I just believe they're
half cracked! and between 'em all, and the hosses
a-falling off, and the everlasting stirring up, my capes is
a-getting as loose as an old blouse!"

And the fat coachman kept on grumbling, but the
roomy coach was kept always bright, the old horses'
groomed as sleek as satin, and the Young Aunties declared that his eyes twinkled in his fat cheeks when
they called him Weller.

Some little time after Aunt Hannah had thus been
restored to the activities of life, her conscience began to
reproach her for her many years of indulgence in solitude and uselessness ; she seemed to feel that she owed
a debt to humanity for her long withdrawal from its
interests and requirements, and she became almost eager
in her quiet way to take up some work by which the
rest of her existence could be made to compensate for
the idle and aimless past. Through contact with other
busy spirits she became cognizant of undeveloped ener-
gies in herself, and she grew restless in her outlook for
some worthy effort. Hitherto she had thought but lit-

tle of her accumulated wealth; her abundance, having
been a matter of habit, had been taken as a matter of
course, and its comings in and its goings out had been
regulated only by her individual needs and luxuries; but
now the burden of her possessions pressed on her, the
inequalities of human fortunes touched her tender soul,
she grew into comprehension of her stewardship, and
longed to find a judicious and beneficial channel into
which to direct her unemployed riches for the helping
and salvation of others.   At last this constant thought
and yearning became almost a trouble to her, and she
must fain open her full heart to the Young Mother and
the wise old Grandmothers, who entered into her feelings and plans with a zest and sympathy all the greater,
perhaps, with one of them, that she felt a little guilty in
her own mind of having made sundry calculations on
the probable distribution of Aunt Hannah's fortune;
but even she was just enough to perceive that the alle-
viation of the many was a higher purpose than the
enriching of the few, and an earnest interest was
yielded to the lonely woman who was so unaffectedly
reaching out to do good.   Then, too, it is a curious
peculiarity of our complicated human nature that the

disappointment of future advantage may be condoned
by present confidence and the privileged pleasure of
co-operation and assistance in the very object which
changes the direction of bestowal; for to be personally
valued by some particular people is often more gratify-
ing than the mere anticipation or reception of their
generosity. So these women held many a disinterested
consultation, discussed scheme after scheme, went
about together to hospitals and asylums, and studied
great charities, if thereby they might light upon the
best thing to be effected—but without success; for all
understood that whatsoever her hand might find to do,
it was Aunt Hannah's wish that she should do it with
her own might, that she desired to absorb her own per-
sonality in it, and pass the rest of her days in service
acceptable to the Lord.

But the Young Mother, having her Baby for inspiration, and having once seen into the depths of that
sensitive heart which had been plunged into solitude by
the deprivation of motherhood, divined at last the
truest direction to satisfy the searching spirit.

"Dear Aunt Hannah," she said one day, when they
were alone, "it seems to me that in the work you are
9

looking for you need something on which you can
expend love as well as money; it is a dry business just
doing a general good without one's own emotions are
exercised at the same time. As a woman, what your
nature is craving is not that wide, vague affection for
all humanity which would make you help just for
humanity's sake; that is very grand, but the glow of it
is too exalted to be continual in one's daily feelings.
You need some little part of humanity to come near to
you as your very own, to cherish and to aid. You
want it in your home, in your every-day life, to fill the
nooks and corners of your hungry heart. And, dear
Auntie, I think there is only one thing that will do all
this for you, for you are one of those women in whom
the mother-instinct is stronger than any other, if you
will only give it a chance. You have no children, and
in this unequal world there are so many, many poor
babies who have no mothers. You have this large,
empty house, and a warm heart ready to take in the
helpless. Fill them with babies. Take into your
loving arms these little waifs that are left unloved, and
I think, dear Auntie, that such a work would be a
blessing to you every way."

Aunt Hannah caught at the idea at once; and the Grandmothers said "it was the very thing!" and they wondered they had not thought of it before; the Grandfathers shrugged their shoulders, and remarked that "all women were mad on the subject of babies!" which observation the Young Aunties immediately proved by expressing their delight in exaggerated adjectives; while the Poor Relation told the Crippled Sister about it with appreciative tears in her soft eyes.

Then into the gray old house were brought little friendless orphans, and the prim footman was kept distractingly busy with the comings in of cribs and cradles and all the other needed paraphernalia of infancy; and in finding her vocation, Aunt Hannah had created a new interest for other lives; the Grandmothers could scarcely bear to stay away from those once empty rooms now made full and vocal; they felt the value of their advice and experience; they trotted about, rosy and important, in the service of these small protégés and more than once bore in their own arms, from the haunts of poverty and the embrace of dead mothers, some helpless babe to the saving refuge of this ready home. The Young Mother's susceptible heart

overflowed with yearning towards the parentless nurs-
lings, and her love for her own Baby made all these
sacred and beautiful and precious in her sight. The
Poor Relation came in among them as one born with
a gift to soothe their sufferings and still their cries, and
the motherhood of her woman's soul developed when
she took these children in her arms and blessed them.
The Fat Nurse found her way there with her mysterious
basket, and was always cordially welcomed, for many
a useful hint was dropped from beneath the coal-scuttle
bonnet, and more than one sage suggestion emphasized
with the bulgy umbrella. But the Young Aunties were
quite absorbed in the new enterprise ; they constituted
themselves amateur nurses, and learned patience in the
labor ; they rocked cradles to the measure of favorite
operas; they picked out particular infants, and gossiped about their beauties with as much relish as over
their beaux ; they discussed the latest arrival as eagerly
as the last fashion ; they knit up pounds upon pounds
of zephyr into warm and fluffy infantile wraps ; and
even the babies' eyes brightened in recognition of their
gay voices and sunny faces ; but through it all, though
others might charm their hearts, their own Baby

reigned supreme fetish still, and the one unrivalled
standard of comparison. Even the Grandfathers
found themselves drawn into the general attraction,
and were occasionally captured and taken triumphantly
through rows of babies in that stirring gray house that
they had so long known in its sombre loneliness, and
were touched into sending wholesale presents of rattles and unlimited supplies of arrow-root, besides allow-
ing themselves amiably to be laid under all sorts
of contributions therefor by the insatiable Young
Aunties, without the usual masculine protest at such
assailing.

In Aunt Hannah herself the change wrought by her
work seemed little less than miraculous; no one would
have known her for the reserved, sorrowful woman she
was before. Her hands and time were so full that silence and solitude were no longer practicable; she had
so much to do that it gave her also a great deal to say,
every faculty was utilized, every energy brought into
play, and she blossomed out into a matronly sweetness
and earnest motherliness that set its impress on her
altered appearance.

Even the prim footman manifested the most unexpected aptitudes under the circumstances; and being the only man in the house with so many unprotected females and their charges, assumed a sort of paternal responsibility whose unction greatly tempered his primness, so that he made shy passes at the babies by chucking them under their chins, and was more than once observed to be slyly dandling a stray infant under the friendly shade of spreading trees in the garden. And the fat coachman was busier than ever—almost too busy to growl, especially as the Young Aunties were too much taken up with the babies that he carefully drove out for their airings, to torment him so unreasonably about imaginary widows.

So Aunt Hannah's Orphan Asylum became a recognized institution, not only in the immediate family, but in the whole appreciating town. It met a great want, and before long grew into proportions never anticipated at first. Little did this gentle woman, who had put her hand so willingly to this work, ever imagine how great the need of it had been, and how many motherless waifs there were to be rescued from unkindness, neglect, and death. Soon the gray old house was too crowded and too small, and it wrung Aunt Hannah's heart to have to turn away into the cold charity of the outside world a single baby that was brought to her door; so first one wing was added, and then another, and more of earth's deserted little ones were gathered into this saving fold. And still they came, more and more, till in this ministry of love even Aunt Hannah's ample resources began to be strained and insufficient for further admittances. And as she pondered over this a little sadly one day, she was accosted by the prim footman in a state of perturbation and embarrassment quite unusual to that worthy servitor.

"If you please, ma'am," he began somewhat hesitatingly and very crimson in the face, "I'd like to say a few words. I've lived with you pretty near all my life, ma'am, and God and yourself willing, hope to die in your service; and not having a chick nor a child of my own, and never expecting to, I've saved up a lot of my wages with no particular purpose; and as I'm as interested in the babies as anybody, and I know, ma'am, begging your pardon, that you've been a-worrying because there ain't room enough, why, I'd just like this money of mine to go towards building a bit or so more.

If you'll please, ma'am, to take it, I'll think it well-earned and well-spent."

And Aunt Hannah was quite overcome with this generosity, but reasoned with James about it, very unwilling to take from him his treasured savings; but the prim footman was not to be denied, and answered firmly, "If I died, ma'am, I should leave my money to this here asylum, and glad of something to do with it, as I've got no kinfolks, and I might as well see the good of it with my living eyes!" So Aunt Hannah comprehended that he would be greatly hurt and disappointed if she refused his assistance; and as the prim footman had had little temptations to spend, his accumulation proved to be larger than might have been supposed, and afforded quite a respectable addition, which was built out towards the garden, and called in his honor "James' Ward." And the delight exhibited thereat by the prim footman was quite a sight to see. He watched every brick and stone with affectionate interest, peered into the lime-kiln, and hovered round the hods; all his leisure was devoted to superintending with intense solicitude the rearing of the walls; he waited on the workmen with untiring zeal, and was

even suspected of having occasionally laid a few lines
of mortar himself; he would hardly sleep in his im
patience and anxiety to see the roof actually on; and
when at last all was finished, and the superfluous
babies had overflowed into the new rooms from the
main building, the prim footman adopted these as his
especial favorites and care, so that at length, to his
supreme enjoyment, they came to be called "James'
Children;" and as time went on, under the combined
effects of busy days and perpetual babies, his primness
all wore away, and he mellowed into a genial sort of
general father, and quite forgetting the dignified
limitations of a footman, was often to be seen in the
long walks of the old-fashioned garden, patiently and
tenderly carrying some ailing infant through the fresh
air, or sitting on his particular bench beneath the
largest tree with one, or even two babies on his knees
playing with the buttons that were worn above such a
kind and faithful heart.

Once, when the needs were many and the laborers
still too few, the Poor Relation was surprised, as she sat
by the Crippled Sister, by a visit from Aunt Hannah,
who simply said to her: "Dear, I have more than I can

9*

do, and require help. You must come to me and be
my right hand." But the Poor Relation only looked
over at the white couch and frail figure, under whose
transparent fingers the white flowers were growing upon
a flowing robe; and Aunt Hannah put her arms around
her and said softly: "Not alone, dear, oh, not alone!
both must come, for there is work and welcome for
both!"

And the Poor Relation, whose humble home had felt
very lonely since the Sunset of Life had fallen on the
Aged Father and Mother, turned to this one of her very
own who was left to her, and asked : "Sister, shall we
go?" And the Crippled Sister dropped the snowy
muslin, and put forth a trembling hand to each, as she
answered with a quivering voice, "Inasmuch as ye do
it to the least of these, my little ones, ye do it unto
Me!" So, a little while afterwards, the Grandfathers
themselves came and carried the Crippled Sister down
to a mattress in the roomy coach, from out of that one
apartment which she had not left for so many years;
and nothing could exceed the carefulness with which
the fat coachman slowly drove over picked ways to the
gray old house, where also were conveyed the white

couch, the blithe bird, and all the other familiar things
upon which her eyes had rested in the olden home;
and in their midst the Crippled Sister still worked on,
only now her skillful hands fashioned only garments
for the babies; and hither followed her, also, her loving
scholars to find increased knowledge in a wider school
of humanity; and all the rest of her days passed away
in such pleasantness and peace as her condition would
admit; and not the Poor Relation only, but Aunt Hannah and all the rest went in to her for that spiritual
strength which seemed to flow in upon her open soul
from the very secret places of the Most High.

Years went on and on; Aunt Hannah's work and
will never faltered. Babies came and came, and the
mother-heart took them all in—took them all in and
cherished and reared them for the life that is, and the
life that is to come. She lived to be an old woman,
with a soul full of wisdom, and her face came to be as
the face of one who had talked with God, with the love
that was in it. And the Young Mother would almost
have thought in time that she had put away the grief
and memories of her youth amid the beautiful interests
of her busy age, if she had not known that always

in that gray old house there was kept a single room
unused, in which there was an empty cradle where no
baby ever slept; and she wondered, sometimes, if,
among all the active concerns of her beneficent life,
she had nourished still the strange doubt which had
tortured the brooding loneliness of that unmentioned
past, for Aunt Hannah never again recurred to the
story of her sorrow. But at last, when the time was
ripe, Aunt Hannah lay upon her dying bed, surrounded
by loving spirits and mourned for by hundreds outside;
when the Young Aunties—some of them also mothers
then—wept bitterly and would not be comforted; when
only the one Grandfather and the one Grandmother
who were left, bent their white heads before the
mystery they too were soon to meet. When Baby's
Nurse paused in her ineffectual ministry, the Young
Mother, who had become a comely matron with Baby
a grown-up young lady at her side, recalled that memorable morning in the long ago, when the lonely woman
had told her with hopeless tears, of the child who had
died before it was born. And lo, as she looked down
upon the pale face resting on the Poor Relation's
gentle bosom, the eyes suddenly opened and looked

into hers; with the failing strength the aged hand caught her own and drew her close, as the last words, which she only completely understood, fell from the lips already cold in death : " I have seen my baby; its face was the face of the *living*, and it had its father's eyes ! "

IX.

BABY could not understand it at all; she only comprehended in her small way that a great change had come over everything in her little world. The dear Young Mother lay very pale and quiet on her bed, and Baby's crib had been removed from her side into the chamber of Baby's Nurse, all of whose tenderness and patience could not supply the loss—when, restless in the new place, Baby woke in the night—of the low, familiar tones, and the soft caress of the maternal hand that always soothed, because Baby knew it so well, and felt such a sense of security and peace under it.

The Fat Nurse had come in one day in her coal-scuttle bonnet, with her bulgy umbrella and never-failing basket. But she had come to stay, for the basket had been deposited in the closet, with its faded green ribbon strings all untied; the umbrella had been carefully stood in a remote corner, and the big bonnet replaced by a stiffly-starched frilled cap that struck awe into Baby's heart; and as somehow Baby dimly connected the arrival of this important personage with the beginning of her troubles, she looked upon that florid countenance with no favorable eye, especially as the Fat Nurse was so absorbed in a white bundle on her lap that she took very little notice of Baby Number One. Nor could Baby see any reason why that same long white bundle should attract the attention of every one who came in almost to the exclusion of Baby's hitherto most prominent self; and the ominous phrase, "Baby's nose is out of joint," so often repeated, seemed to imply some usurpation of her infantile rights, and such a relegation to the background, that when the Fat Nurse at last condescended to hold the white bundle low down for her sisterly inspection, her only impulse was to double her dimpled fist and make an effort to punch the tiny bald head suddenly presented to her bewildered view.

First, when Baby's Nurse had brought her in fresh and rosy from her bath, to receive the Young Mother's languid morning kiss, this new-comer had been held

up for due observance, and Baby's Nurse had clasped
her close to her breast, and said " Baby's nose is out of
joint " with such a sad inflection in her voice, that
Baby felt that some misfortune had befallen her, and
that this white doll with the scarlet face was the occasion of it. And the Fat Nurse had responded, " Turn
about, fair play! " in such an unsympathetic tone, that
Baby hated her forthwith.

Then the Young Father had come in, and was very
tender over his pale wife, and passing Baby by, had
gone across the room, and leaned over the new child,
looking at it silently for a moment, touching its downy
cheek gently with his finger, and then, as Baby keenly
felt, with his notice only partly engrossed by her, had
taken her in his arms for the usual greeting and toss,
exclaiming half abstractedly and half triumphantly,
" Baby's nose is out of joint! " Baby's nose began to
have a queer sensation, and was very nearly twisted for
a burst of crying, as the Fat Nurse replied: " It's
natur' sir! Babies comes and babies goes, and noses
ain't steady long." The Young Father laughed a
happy little laugh, and went off to his office with his
heart brimming over with joy at the Young Mother's

safety, and the addition of another darling to his household, and left Baby feeling more and more that the
Fat Nurse was her mortal enemy.

Then Baby had been banished from the Young
Mother's room, which had been her only nursery, to
another afar off, where she vented herself for two or
three days in all the ill-tempers of babyhood ; and
when she was just about to find consolation in a bald-
pated dolly that had a towel pinned round it to repre-
sent the white bundle down stairs, and which she
could shake and slap to her heart's content, she was
suddenly called for .to go and see the Grandfathers,
who had come to welcome their last grandchild into
this mortal world. And lo ! as she entered at the door
Grandfather Number Two shook his gold-headed cane
as if he was threatening her, and called out lustily :
"Ha ! ha ! little one, your nose is out of joint ! " and
Grandfather Number One echoed the phrase just
a shade less forcibly. And the Fat Nurse began to
trot down a rising whine from the new-found voice,
accompanying the motion with the refrain, "Out of
joint, out of jointy, jointy, jointy, joint ! " So that
when, in a new accession of wrath, Baby declined to be

received upon the Grandpaternal knees, the ancient men chucked her under the chin, and smiling at each other as if it was a good joke, said merrily : " The little vixen is jealous !" and Baby experienced for the first time that Grandfathers are a delusion and a snare.

The Grandmothers rustled in, with their rosy faces and shining black silks, and chirruped to the Young Mother, and gossiped over the new baby, with just a careless kiss to Baby, who began to watch with sensitive spirit for tokens of inattention and displacement, till at last one of them, laying her hand upon the golden curls, said conclusively: ." Well, Nurse, it is a very fine child, and this one's nose is out of joint!" And the Fat Nurse, like an everlasting echo, had responded: "Every dog must have his day!" And Baby turned her large eyes reproachfully upon the frilled cap, as if wondering why, when her old friend had removed her big bonnet, she should thus take part with every one against her former nursling.

The roomy coach, driven by the Fat Coachman, brought Aunt Hannah to the unusually quiet house, where the missing of the sweet presence going in and out of the rooms gave all but the one an aspect of lone-

liness and emptiness. She had taken the new baby in
her arms, and sat holding it awhile with her face full
of blessing and love; Baby stood a little way off, looking at her wistfully, and waiting for the inevitable remark, and then, as if magnetized by the yearning that
softened the brooding features, she slowly drew anear,
and leaned up against her. Quickly one arm was disen-
gaged from the white bundle, and went around the
small figure not too steadfast yet upon its chubby feet,
and the thoughtful eyes were turned upon the almost im-
ploring little countenance lifted to her own, and Aunt
Hannah saw there something that no one else had observed, for she said, half-questioningly, " I wonder if
this wee creature feels that her pretty nose is out of
joint ? " to which the Fat Nurse heartlessly replied,
"I reckon she's most too young to feel much yet, and
anyhow, she'll soon get used to it ! " Poor Baby began
to have a dim perception that there was no longer any
hope for her, and that the repetition of this bitter phrase
spread desolation over her early days. The bright
Young Aunties floated in, gay and gushing over the
great event; and they cooed, and gurgled, and talked
baby talk over the strange arrival, and tenderly touch-

ed its mites of hands, and insisted on being shown its
tinted feet and tiny toes, till Baby's heart swelled within her, for perhaps she remembered, as it was not so
long ago, that they had once gone on in the same way
over her now neglected self. It was too much that this
red-faced, bald-headed bundle should rob her of the
allegiance of these devoted adherents; too much that
the flattery of their ringing voices should be turned
aside from their hitherto spoiled and reigning darling;
that the pet names should be transferred and the faith-
less admiration changed to a new object. What to the
grown woman is the misery of power and love passing
away to a rival, was Baby's experience of this fickleness
of adulation; her small brow puckered, and her rose-
bud of a mouth began to quiver; and as a woman ex-
erts all her arts to win back again the waning influence,
so the undeveloped cunning of womanhood born in an
infant's breast, caused Baby to put forth all her hitherto irresistible wiles to attract the altered attention.
And the Young Aunties saw through the device and
made themselves merry over it, and petted her fondly,
but with a side glance still at the new baby; and as
though conscious of a diminished interest in their here-

tofore idol, passed her from one to another with a manner that was partly self-excusing, as each said to each, " But our Baby's nose is out of joint ! "

The childish heart was very full, but not yet did the cup overflow, until the Poor Relation entered the room, and catching a glimpse of the young face with the shadow of a first sorrow on it, murmured as though she comprehended the situation, " Ah ! the poor little nose is out of joint." That was the last drop ! That she too, the best beloved, should echo this unceasing reproach, and sting the suffering soul with these repeated words of doom, even though spoken in compassion, was more than could be longer endured. Then Baby went quickly aside, and turning her face from all of them, sat down in a distant corner fronting the wall, and great sobs rose in her throat, and the moans of a bruised spirit sounded through the surprised silence. Consternation fell for a moment upon every one present; but the Fat Nurse, so careless before, divined the meaning of this outburst.

" I do believe," she said remorsefully, " that we've all been blind' as bats and hard as rocks, and that that Baby has been a-thinkin' and a-feelin' more than we had any idea of! Every one of us has been a-tellin' her that her nose is out of joint, till it has made the little creetur' lonesome. We don't give these young uns credit enough for knowinness. Poor little tot!"

But the Young Mother had risen up in bed, and cried out: "Oh, give me my Baby!—not that one—my first Baby! Don't you see her heart is breaking! Oh, bring her to me!"

And the Poor Relation lifted the little desolate form in her gentle arms and laid her on the Young Mother's bosom, where the passionately tender words and the soft, familiar caress soon stilled the strangling sobs and grief-wrung wail; and sheltered there upon that faithful breast, Baby gained her first conception and réalization that, come weal or woe, though friends may fail and the world forget, or others share the sacred love, to the Mother's heart no Baby's nose is ever out of joint.

X.

Baby was over two years old, and was no longer Baby; another little one had come into her infantile place, and in the changes and chances of this mortal life Baby had come to be known by her own name—the beloved and blessed name of the Poor Relation. To the gay and gushing young girls she was no longer the sole and undivided ·Pet; and that One of the Aunties, whom she had saved for her husband, had now a baby of her own. Baby's Nurse shared her care and love with another charge, and Baby's Party had become a tale of tradition. The Crippled Sister had found the sweetness of living in working out her tender fancies on the white robes for Aunt Hannah's Orphan Asylum; and since the Sunset of Life had fallen on the humble home where the Aged Father and Mother had sat for the last time in the vine-wreathed porch, the Poor Rela-

tion had keenly felt that nothing in this world is
stationary; and that over individual and family, as
well as through the fortunes of the Great Many, irresistible Time was forever bringing alteration and move-
ment. But though Baby might be compensated for
the loss of separate idolatry by the welcome companionship of other babies, and though the woman's
sphere might be enlarged by more numerous duties
and wider interests, yet perhaps in Baby's little heart
there might have been an undefined sense of something
missing and gone, as in the woman's soul there was an
unconquerable clinging to things of the past.

She was thinking much in this strain as she wended
her way across the fields where she had found the five-
leaved clover, to pay a last visit to her old home, which,
in the course of events, was about to pass out of her
possession; and she was going to stand once more in
the familiar rooms, long sanctified by sacrifice and
suffering, to weep her full heart out alone beneath the
roof that had sheltered her nearest and dearest, and to
bid a sad farewell to the sacred walls, the cherished
flowers, the precious associations of the abandoned
abode of many years. It might be lowly in the sight

of others, but no place or palace on earth could ever
be so sweet and beautiful to her, because of the kindred lives that had been spent and finished there.

She was thinking nothing now of five-leaved clovers
or Fairy Gifts; her innermost spirit was all stirred
with memories, and she was dwelling far more on
those who had gone before to the unknown bourne,
than of the new-born existences to which she was herself, in very truth, a Fairy Godmother. Titania and
Puck had no place in the mind that was busy with the
angels in heaven; the Fairy Court could not enter into
the musings on an empty hearth, and the Rose of Life
and Lily of Death had become to her only a part of
a lovely dream in which Fancy had played with the
secret things of humanity. Long and solemn was the
vigil she had set for herself in the silent house; very
still and solitary would the hours of the night be in
this dwelling of perished hopes and vanished labors;
but she knew that the Voices of the Past would speak
to her soul, and that she would hold communion with
the invisible.

The outer door, through which those she loved would
go back and forth no more, swung back slowly as
10

though loth to admit her to the darkness and loneliness; the walls that would so soon resound with the tones of strangers gave back a faint and mournful echo of her lingering steps; and the very windows seemed to lean over and look down upon her sympathetically, as if she only was their own. Ah! what thoughts, what homely remembrances, what irrepressible yearnings filled those parting hours, when the dumb and senseless wood and plaster even seemed to be permeated with the personal influences that had emanated in their midst, and to give back the concentrated impression of vanished presences. The bitterness of death was in the unseen wringings of the hands; the awful cry of the human in the moan unheard of men; and the saltness of mortal suffering in the tears which fell in the deserted dwelling! Ghosts were there, but she had no fear of them; the dead arose from their graves and came noiselessly about her, but she shrank not from their companionship, for to her beautiful faith they wore the wings of God's Messengers, and it was not for them the rain of grief fell down, but for her own coming years upon earth below without their outward and visible intercourse. For though the trained spirit may willingly murmur "Thy will Be Done," there is no reconciliation in the heart, which remains always natural, with sorrow and bereavement.

She came down at last as the clock was striking midnight, to stand within the vine-wreathed porch, beneath the starry sky, to look out once more upon the flower-decked lawn all bright and silvered with the summer moonlight.

At the first stroke of the church-bell, to whose tolling of the hours she had so often listened in the night-watches, a rustling breeze stirred all the clustering leaves; at the third stroke it suddenly seemed to her swimming eyes as if all the flowers on the vines expanded at once into full bloom, and turned upon their stems towards the lawn; at the fifth stroke innumerable fire-flies paled with their restless brilliancy the softer moonshine; at the seventh the dewy grass and bushes sparkled as if sprinkled with diamonds; at the ninth stroke the blossoms distilled a flood of marvellous fragrance; at the eleventh a slender white circle appeared instantaneously before her, flashing into her mind the remembrance of the five-leaved clover; and at the

twelfth stroke, there straightway before her was truly
all the Fairy Court!

The Poor Relation was greatly amazed, for she had
no charm now with which to summon the little people,
and had often doubted whether she had once really beheld and talked with the tiny Queen of the Elves. Only
when, day by day she had watched Baby growing into
the good gifts which she fancied were bestowed upon
her on a certain memorable night, did she sometimes
allow herself to dwell on the belief that she, even she
had won from the fays these blessings for the general
darling. But the practical things of every-day existence, crowding thick and fast, thrust down into the
secret place of her heart the lingering childishness
which delighted to muse on poetic visions of storied
sprites. And she had told no one that she had held
converse with the Fairies, for she knew that the incred-
ulity of To-day would have impugned her sanity, and
this same skepticism of the outer life, which is Common
Sense, had so far stolen into her Inner Me, that until
she beheld them all before her again she had come to
think that her former interview was an illusion of
rarely indulged imagination.

But there they all unmistakably were once more, and she knew that her fancy had no part in their appearance now, since it was of far other glorified beings she had been thinking, than these gossamer and airy creatures. And she could not but notice that this time they wore no guise of lightness or merriment. Titania, seated on her white rose throne, looked grave and solemn, while her silvery robe was mistier than before, and the crown of minute jewels upon her brow seemed dim and heavy. Puck drooped dejectedly, and made no sly passes at the quiet pages; and over all the liliputian assembly there reigned an aspect of depression and distress.

After a moment's silence Titania sadly spoke:

"Because, O gentle spirit! that you were the last in the land who kept faith in us, we came to you before—we, who were once summoned to the christening feasts of all the princes of the world; but since you too have let belief grow cold, and have permitted yourself to think of us as creatures of fiction, we must bid you farewell forever!"

"Ah, no!" cried the Poor Relation, "for now that I see you again my faith comes back, and I know you all for the veritable fairies that my childhood longed to see ! "

" Yes," said Titania a little scornfully, " just now it is night, and you are alone, and we are here; but to-morrow, in the broad day, will you dare to proclaim aloud in the market-place that we really do exist, and that you have seen us with your natural eyes, and heard us with your conscious ears ? "

And the Common Sense, which is so cruel a foe to Genius, 'and so staunch an ally to Truth, caused the Poor Relation to keep silent and slightly hang her head in shame, and the bright ring of fairies all sighed so piteously that she felt very culpable indeed.

" Ah well ! " continued Titania, " we can pardon you, for the Spirit of the Age has inherited our lost power, and its impressions are stronger than we, since they only can endure the glare of the sunshine, while we are the children of the shadows and the Past. There is no place for us any longer in this country of steam and schools ; but as long as one heart remained that cherished us we lingered in our olden haunts. But we have bidden them all adieu—even as you have bidden adieu to your former home—with all the grief that fairies ever can feel, and now we have come to add one more farewell to-night to those you and we have already taken."

"But, O Queen!" exclaimed the Poor Relation, "why must you go? why must the places which have known you so long know you now no more?"

"Can you not understand," replied Titania almost sharply, "that when knowledge comes, the fairies must go? In this very house, have there not been gathered in the ignorant children, whose parents brought with them from a far country all the traditions of our rule, to be shown the light of science and taught the power of fact? When a child has pulled a flower to pieces in order to count the pistils and stamens, do you think she will ever again see a fairy peeping from its leaves? Your locomotives have cut through our meadow circles where we danced so merrily of yore; your railroads have tunnelled the hills whose recesses were all Fairy Land, invisible to the spade and measuring-line; and the very woods beneath whose shady ferns we slept so securely in the day-time, have been cut down for Telegraph poles, and there is no longer any suitable spot in this wretched land of bare actuality, work, and progress, for beings so delicate and ethereal as we ! "

And a low wail, like the dying fall of the wind at night, went up from the saddened Fairy Court.

" But where will you go, oh, where will you go ? " asked the Poor Relation ; " for though you should again fade away from me as realities, your memories will not pass from my heart, and I would fain picture you in whatsoever region you may be ! "

" We will go," answered Titania slowly, " to some . barbaric land whose people are still children; where the eyes have not been dulled by education, nor where ears have grown deaf to the voices of nature. For them we will dance again in the moonlight, and people their glens and glades ; they will see us amid the ferns, and find our circles in the fields ; and we will be happier with them than we have been for a long time here, for with much knowledge cometh much sorrow to man as well as to fairies ! "

Then the Poor Relation stretched her arms to the little people. "I know," she said, " O beautiful Queen ! that you and yours will never quite go out of my life. I may never again see you with the eyes of

my sense, but wherever you may go my soul will summon you again and again, and you will come from the
far away, and whisper to me of the new worlds you
have found, pour sweet fancies into my innermost
longings, and gather around me in the silence of sleep
and night!"

"Ah ha!" cried Puck, "she believes in us yet!
There is enough of the child left in the woman to hold
us dear still!   Must we go while one heart so clings to
us?"

And all the small elves echoed anxiously, "Must we
go? must we go?"

But Titania answered mournfully, "It is true that
we can never quite forsake those who love us; but we
must go, alas! we must go from this civilization to
which she belongs, if we are to live at all, for the
March of Improvement treads down such as we, and
advancing Reason accounts it good to look upon us
slain!   And even she will consider that Use is better
than Beauty, and help to train up that Baby which we
gifted in the New Order of Things that will know us
no more!   But because she only, for so long in the
midst of All This, has cherished us and summoned us,
10*

and will regret us, we will leave her a gift which shall remain forever fresh in her heart, to which we will sometimes secretly return."

And then it seemed to the Poor Relation that all the Fairy Court ringed her round, floating in the mid-air; that they touched her with their tiny hands, and kissed her with their little, little mouths; and that Titania, pausing a moment in front of her, left an offering lying on her breast. Then a cloud swept over the face of the moon, and when it had passed away the little people had all gone out of sight forever; but still upon the scented breeze there swelled the melancholy cadence of their last "Farewell!" And as she glanced downward she saw through her involuntary tears a single familiar flower lying on her bosom within the folds of her dress; and all her life long the Poor Relation always knew that any one to whom, in the night of sorrow or amid the hours of care, the fairies could come unbidden, or who could behold a vision of Titania, would never be entirely left alone in the darkness without this token of Heart's-ease.

THE END.

1877.   1877.

NEW BOOKS

AND. NEW EDITIONS,

RECENTLY ISSUED BY

G. W. CARLETON & Co., Publishers,

Madison Square, New York.

———o———

The Publishers, upon receipt of the price in advance, will send any book on this Catalogue by mail, *postage free*, to any part of the United States.

———o———

All books in this list [unless otherwise specified] are handsomely bound in cloth board binding, with gilt backs, suitable for libraries.

———o———

Mrs. Mary J. Holmes' Works.

Tempest and Sunshine.........	$1 50	Darkness and Daylight.........	$1 50
English Orphans...	1 50	Hugh Worthington.............	1 50
Homestead on the Hillside....	1 50	Cameron Pride..................	1 50
'Lena Rivers....................	1 50	Rose Mather....................	1 50
Meadow Brook..................	1 50	Ethelyn's Mistake.............	1 50
Dora Deane.............	1 50	Millbank.......................	1 50
Cousin Maude..................	1 50	Edna Browning.................	1 50
Marian Grey....	1 50	West Lawn........(New)........	1 50
Edith Lyle........(New)..........	1 50		

Marion Harland's Works.

Alone.......................	$1 50	Sunnybank.....................	$1 50
Hidden Path..................	1 50	Husbands and Homes...........	1 50
Moss Side....	1 50	Ruby's Husband................	1 50
Nemesis......................	1 50	Phemie's Temptation..........	1 50
Miriam.......................	1 50	The Empty Heart...	1 50
At Last...	1 50	Jessamine.....................	1 50
Helen Gardner................	1 50	From My Youth Up...........	1 50
True as Steel......(New)........	1 50	My Little Love. ....(New).......	1 50

Charles Dickens—15 Vols.—"Carleton's Edition."

Pickwick, and Catalogue......	$1 50	David Copperfield..............	$1 50
Dombey and Son.............	1 50	Nicholas Nickleby.............	1 50
Bleak House..........	1 50	Little Dorrit...................	1 50
Martin Chuzzlewit....-.	1 50	Our Mutual Friend...	1 50
Barnaby Rudge—Edwin Drood..	1 50	Curiosity Shop—Miscellaneous..	1 50
Child's England—Miscellaneous.	1 50	Sketches by Boz—Hard Times....	1 50
Oliver Twist—and—The Uncommercial Traveler			1 50
Great Expectations—and—Pictures of Italy and America...............			1 50
Christmas Books—and—A Tale of Two Cities.			1 50
Sets of Dickens' Complete Works, in 15 vols.—[elegant half calf bindings].			60 00

Augusta J. Evans' Novels.

Beulah..	$1 75	St. Elmo.........	$2 00
Macaria	1 75	Vashti.........................	2 00
Inez.	1 75	Infelice......... ...(New).........	2 00

Miriam Coles Harris.

Rutledge...........................$1 50	The Sutherlands................$1 50
Frank Warrington..... .... 1 50	St. Philip's....................... 1 50
Louie's Last Term, etc.......... 1 50	Round Hearts, for Children..... 1 50
Richard Vandermarck............ 1 50	A Perfect Adonis. (New)........ 1 50

May Agnes Fleming's Novels.

Guy Earlscourt's Wife..........$1 75	A Wonderful Woman...........$1 75
A Terrible Secret................. 1 75	A Mad Marriage........... .... 1 75
Norine's Revenge................. 1 75	One Night's Mystery............ 1 75
A New Book	Kate Danton. (New)............. 1 75

Grace Mortimer.

The Two Barbaras.—A novel ...$1 50 | Bosom Foes. (In press) $1 50

Julie P. Smith's Novels.

Widow Goldsmith's Daughter..$1 75	The Widower...................$1 75
Chris and Otho...................1 75	The Married Belle..... .... 1 75
Ten Old Maids................... 1 75	Courting and Farming............ 1 75
His Young Wife. (New)........ 1 75	

Captain Mayne Reid—Illustrated.

The Scalp Hunters..............$1 50	The White Chief................$1 50
The Rifle Rangers.............. 1 50	The Tiger Hunter................ 1 50
The War Trail................... 1 50	The Hunter's Feast.............. 1 50
The Wood Rangers.............. 1 50	Wild Life........................ 1 50
The Wild Huntress.............. 1 50	Osceola, the Seminole.......... 1 50

A. S. Roe's Select Stories.

True to the Last................$1 50	A Long Look Ahead.......... $1 50
The Star and the Cloud......... 1 50	I've Been Thinking.............. 1 50
How Could He Help It|?........ 1 50	To Love and to be Loved....... 1 50

Charles Dickens.

Child's History of England.—Carleton's New *"School Edition."* Illustrated..$1 25

Hand-Books of Society.

Habits of Good Society.—The nice points of taste and good manners..........$1 50
Art of Conversation.—For those who wish to be agreeable talkers or listeners.... 1 50
Arts of Writing, Reading, and Speaking.—For self-improvement............ 1 50
New Diamond Edition.—Small size, elegantly bound, 3 volumes in a box...... 3 00

Mrs. Hill's Cook Book.

Mrs. A. P. Hill's New Cookery Book, and family domestic receipts.........$2 00

Famous Books—"Carleton's Edition."

Robinson Crusoe.—New 12mo edition, with illustrations by ERNEST GRISET....$1 50
Swiss Family Robinson.—New 12mo edition, with illustrations by MARCKL.... 1 50
The Arabian Nights.—New 12mo edition, with illustrations by DEMORAINE..... 1 50
Don Quixote.—New 12mo edition, with illustrations by GUSTAVE DORÉ.......... 1 50

Victor Hugo.

Les Miserables.—An English translation from the original French. Octavo.....$2 50
Les Miserables.—In the Spanish Language. Two volumes, cloth bound....... 5 00

Popular Italian Novels.

Doctor Antonio.—A love story of Italy. By Ruffini $1 75
Beatrice Cenci.—By Guerrazzi. With a steel engraving from Guido's Picture.... 1 75

M. Michelet's Remarkable Works.

Love (L'amour).—English translation from the original French...............$1 50
Woman (La Femme).—.....Do........Do........Do.................... 1 50

Joaquin Miller.

The One Fair Woman.—A new novel, the scene laid chiefly in Italy...........$2 00

Joseph Rodman Drake.

The Culprit Fay.—The well-known fairy poem, with 100 illustrations............$2 00

Artemus Ward's Comic Works.

A New Stereotype Edition.—Embracing the whole of his writings, with a Biography of the author, and profusely illustrated by various artists $2 00

Josh Billings.

A New Stereotype Edition of the complete writings of Josh Billings. Four vols. in one, with Biography, steel portrait, and 100 comic illustrations........ $2 00

Bessie Turner.

A Woman in the Case.—A new novel, with photographic portrait of author... $1 50

Wm. P. Talboys.

West India Pickles.—Journal of a Winter Yacht Cruise, with illustrations $1 50

Dr. A. K. Gardner.

Our Children.—A Hand-book for the Instruction of Parents and Guardians......$2 00

C. H. Webb (John Paul).

Parodies and Poems............$1 50 | My Vacation.—Sea and Shore.....$1 50

Livingston Hopkins.

Comic Centennial History of the United States.—Profusely Illustrated.....$1 50

Allan Pinkerton.

The Model Town, etc........... $1 50 | A New Book. (In press)..... ..$1 50

Mrs. M. V. Victor.

Passing the Portal.—A new story.$1 50 | A New Book. (In press)........$1 50

Ernest Renan's French Works.

The Life of Jesus................$1 75 | The Life of St. Paul... ....$1 75
Lives of the Apostles............ 1 75 | The Bible in India.—By Jacolliot..2 00

Geo. W. Carleton.

Our Artist in Cuba.—Pictures.....$1 50 | Our Artist in Africa. (In press)..$1 50
Our Artist in Peru.   Do. .... 1 50 | Our Artist in Mexico. Do. .. 1 50

Verdant Green.

A racy English college story—with numerous original comic illustrations......$1 50

Algernon Charles Swinburne.

Laus Veneris, and Other Poems.—An elegant new edition, on tinted paper...$1 50
French Love-Songs.—Selected from the best French authors................... 1 50

Robert Dale Owen.

The Debatable Land Between this World and the Next........ ....$2 00
Threading My Way.—Twenty-five years of Autobiography..... .... 1 50

The Game of Whist.

Pole on Whist.—The late English standard work. New enlarged edition... .. $1 00

Mother Goose Set to Music.

Mother Goose Melodies.—With music for singing, and many illustrations......$1 50

M. M. Pomeroy ("Brick.")

Sense—(a serious book)..... ....$1 50 | Nonsense—(a comic book)..........$1 50
Gold-Dust Do.   .... 1 50 | Brick-Dust Do 1 50
Our Saturday Nights............ 1 50 | Home Harmonies. (In press).... 1 50

Celia E. Gardner's Novels.

Stolen Waters—(in verse).........$1 50 | Tested..................(in prose).$1 75
Broken Dreams Do.   .... 1 50 | Rich Medway's Two Loves. Do.. 1 75
A New Novel. (In press)........ 1 50

Mrs. N. S. Emerson.

Betsey and I are Out.— Poems...$1 50 | Little Folks' Letters.—Prose.....$1 50

Louisa M. Alcott.

Morning Glories—A beautiful child's book, by the author of " Little Women."..,.. $1 50

Geo. A. Crofutt.

Trans-Continental Tourist from New York to San Francisco.—Illustrated..$1 50

Miscellaneous Works.

Johnny Ludlow.—A collection of entertaining English stories............ ..... $1 50
Glimpses of the Supernatural.—Facts, Records, and Traditions...........:.... 2 00
Fanny Fern Memorials.—With a Biography by James Parton.................. 2 00
How to Make Money; and How to Keep It.—By Thomas A. Davies.......... 1 50
Tales From the Operas.—A collection of Stories based upon the opera plots.... 1 50
New Nonsense Rhymes.—By W. H. Beckett, with illustrations by C. G. Bush.. 1 00
Wood's Guide to the City of New York.—Beautifully illustrated........... 1 00
The Art of Amusing.—A book of home amusements, with illustrations...:...... 1 50
A Book About Lawyers.—A curious and interesting volume. By Jeaffreson.... 2 00
A Book About Doctors.   Do.   •   Do.   Do. 2 00
The Birth and Triumph of Love.—Full of exquisite tinted illustrations....... 1 00
Progressive Petticoats.—A satirical tale by Robert B. Roosevelt.............. 1 50
Ecce Femina; or, the Woman Zoe.—Cuyler Pine, author "Mary Brandegee." 1 50
Souvenirs of Travel.—By Madame Octavia Walton Le Vert................... 2 00
Woman, Love and Marriage.—A spicy little work by Fred Saunders......... 1 50
Shiftless Folks.—A brilliant new novel by Fannie Smith.................. 1 75
A Woman in Armor.—A powerful new novel by Mary Hartwell............. 1 50
The Fall of Man.—A Darwinian satire. Author of "New Gospel of Peace.".... 50
The Chronicles of Gotham.—A modern satire. Do.   Do.   25
The Story of a Summer.—Journal Leaves by Cecelia Cleveland.............. 1 50
Phemie Frost's Experiences.—By Mrs Ann S. Stephens 1 75
Bill Arp's Peace Papers.—Full of comic illustrations...................... 1 50
A Book of Epitaphs.—Amusing, quaint, and curious....(New)............... 1 50
Ballad of Lord Bateman.—With illustrations by Cruikshank, (paper).... 25
The Yachtman's Primer.—For amateur sailors. T. R. Warren, (paper). 50
Rural Architecture.—By M. Field. With plans and illustrations.............. 2 00
What I Know of Farming.—By Horace Greeley;...................... 1 50
Transformation Scenes in the United States.—By Hiram Fuller......... 1 50
Marguerite's Journal.—Story for girls. Introduction by author "Rutledge."... 1 50
Kingsbury Sketches.—Pine Grove doings, by John H. Kingsbury. Illustrated.. 1 50

Miscellaneous Novels.

Led Astray.—By Octave Feuillet.. $1 75	Saint Leger.—Richard B. Kimball. $1 75
She Loved Him Madly.—Borys.. 1 75	Was He Successful?.........Do. 1 75
Through Thick and Thin.—Mery. 1 75	Undercurrents of Wall St. Do. 1 75
So Fair Yet False.—Chavette..... 1 75	Romance of Student Life....Do. 1 50
A Fatal Passion.—Bomard........ 1 75	Life in San Domingo.......Do. 1 50
Manfred.—F. D. Guerazzi.......... 1 75	Henry Powers, Banker ......Do. 1 75
Seen and Unseen...... ...... 1 50	To-Day....................Do. 1 75
Purple and Fine Linen.—Fawcett.. 1 75	Bessie Wilmerton.—Westcott..... 1 75
Asses' Ears.............. Do. 1 75	Cachet.—Mrs. M. J. R. Hamilton.. 1 75
A Charming Widow.—Macquoid. 1 75	Romance of Railroad.—Smith..... 1 50
True to Him Ever.—By F. W. R.. 1 50	Fairfax.—John Esten Cooke........ 1 50
The Forgiving Kiss.—By M. Loth. 1 75	Hilt to Hilt. Do. 1 50
Loyal Unto Death.................. 1 75	Out of the Foam. Do. 1 50
Kenneth, My King.—S. A. Brock.. 1 75	Hammer and Rapier.Do. 1 50
Heart Hungry.—M. J.Westmoreland 1 75	Warwick.—By M. T. Walworth.... 1 75
Clifford Troupe. Do. 1 75	Lulu. Do. 1 75
Silcott Mill.—Mrs. Deslonde..... 1 75	Hotspur. Do. 1 75
Ebon and Gold.—C. L. McIlvain.. 1 50	Stormcliff. Do. ... 1 75
Robert Greathouse.—J. F. Swift.. 2 00	Delaplaine. Do. 1 75
Charette 1 50	Beverly, Do. ... 1 75

Miscellaneous Works.

Beldazzle's Bachelor Studies....$1 00	Northern Ballads.—Anderson.... $1 00
Little Wanderers.—Illustrated... 1 50	O. C. Kerr Papers. 4 vols. in 1..... 2 00
Genesis Disclosed.—T. A. Davies.. 1 50	Victor Hugo.—His life............. 2 00
Commodore Rollingpin's Log... 1 50	Beauty is Power................. 1 50
Brazen Gates.—A juvenile........ 1 50	Sandwiches.—Artemus Ward..... 25
Antidote to Gates Ajar.......... 25	Widow Spriggins.—Widow Bedott. 1 75
The Snoblace Ball.............. 25	Squibob Papers.—John Phœnix.... 1 50

www.ingramcontent.com/pod-product-compliance
Lightning Source LLC
Chambersburg PA
CBHW030109030726
47498CB00007B/2310